WAKING ROE

STORIES AND POEMS IN HONOR OF CHOICE

AMY A. DECEW

WAKING ROE

Dedication

For all of those who came before, who fought for choice.

For all of those who want choice now, fighting still.

And for those who come after,
keeping choice America's choice once again.

Contents

Introduction

To the people of the United States of America seeking reproductive freedom, I am so, so sorry. If I could wave a wand and be your fairy godmother, you would have chances and choices far better than what we face now. Especially for the women of reproductive age, and that includes more age ranges than an outdated set of statistics often considers, this time is a gruesome about-face that I feel disgraced by. And realize how easily, through violence and a lack of legal rights or money, I could become just one more victim of a nation on the march backward through a history that never had to be repeated.

For those who have chosen to vote for the bodily and medical autonomy of women, in referendum after ballot measure after special election; thank you. You provided a rebuke to the genderized theft of freedoms that some of our mothers were allowed, that many of us are now denied. The overall situation in the U.S. causes me to question how fast we'll spin backward into even more extremist, outdated mandates. This nation has been on a bad tear, and it is only the American people who can bring it back into balance. Will we, and on what? For whom?

The Dobbs decision, though not unexpected, horrified me. What follows in this small book are reflections in grief, anger, and absurdist mockery that reveal my overwhelming disgust with where we are now on the issue of reproductive rights in America.

It's meant to be a home for those who feel that this is a tragic and outrageous situation that no nation claiming to be global leader in equality would ever permit. I know you're in touch with others who share your rage and dismay; we share that together. And there is too little focus on what we share, if, in fact, we share anything at all anymore, America. This issue in particular has put a renewed emphasis on what, surprisingly in today's "United" States, many of us do agree about.

We all come from different walks, but can we walk together now to make this better for women who want the same reproductive and healthcare rights as men? We have heard horrendous tales from twenty-first century women, stories that belong in some past epoch, yet stories that are now.

How surreal is this landscape, and here in this book, how much more ludicrous could I make it? If this nation is going to take reproductive rights to dignity-smashing, sanity-bashing, science-denying real-world extremes that people are forced to live, then I will take this into the realm not only of reflection, but also of completely ridiculous and simply raging. Because America, aren't you?

The issue is not just for women, and neither is the book, as there are many pro-choice men out there. Thank you, and we need your help. We need everyone who cares, of whatever gender, about the ability of a so-called democracy with so-called representation to cut one gender out of the options another one has always had.

I write about topics that are controversial, so this is your warning sign. Don't go any further if you are in a fragile state. While I mostly use the larger situation and myself as the hero-antihero-weirdo characters, there are very serious life situations and questions that can be offensive to some or emotional for others.

For example, I write in language that includes profanity. Additionally, since we're having new conversations about suicide and mental health, that's included. Like you, I can't ignore or deny the tremendous rates of all kinds of violence in this country. And I have lived through horrendous medical outcomes that will leave me damaged for the rest of my life. I'm tired of my expected silence on all of it, this larger landscape that we are all living through, but I'm used to being told to shut up about it. That's never worked yet, so keep that in mind.

You should also know that while none of the content goes into extensive medical detail, nor is pornographic, there are anatomical and procedure mentions. Bit difficult to write the book without those. Additionally, reproductive rights are a sensitive, complex topic for adults. Preferably, adults with compassion.

I don't know about you, but I find that's the most lacking quality of the nation that calls itself "the greatest". Compassion is never viewed as wisdom. Not on this issue and not on any others, as far as I can tell. How far will you take that, America, on this priority and so much more? This nation has taken my reproductive rights right off a cliff. I have to ask, what's next?

Chapter One

Back to Whose Future?

Poem: Justice(s)

Three in the sky and such clear ground, and all we could hear was a whispering sound of something come creeping to seize what we thought; we aimed and we missed but we had two more shots.

Two in the sky and one on the ground, and all we could hear was a whistling sound of the crypt come screaming in, hellfire-hot; we aimed and we missed but we had one more shot.

One in the sky and two on the ground and all we could hear was a whirlwind of sound of the earth in craters as we cratered the lot; we aimed and we missed and it was our last shot.

None in the sky and three on the ground and all we could hear was a wailing sound of a nation gone missing in violence and rot; we'd aimed and we missed and we blew our last shot.

So much for the sky, so much for the ground, so much for hearing just one more sound as the silence set still what our blood had bought; the end of our women, like it or not.

***

Story: Roe is Dead. Long Live Roe.

They stabbed her in the back and buried her in a shallow grave, carving slurs into her corpse skin as they burned her sisters alive in their homes, barring the doors and dousing them with gasoline to send the flames higher, faster. They ran away laughing, flying their flags of tyrants and traitors, the ones they owed their allegiance and treasure vaults to. Then they locked the rest in churches and prisons, and set about as armies do in war, of raping their enemies, these enemies they'd made of women and the men who will defend women's bodies from pillage.

No one was spared. Pockets of the country organized around the fifty-year precedent took measures to preserve it, enshrine it, to give life to their dead heroine. Other places, long the backward ones, fired up effigies of the precedent and seized every paper, torching it all in the rampage of hate and ignorance that the swaggering braggart nation had become.

Or so were my thoughts on June 24, 2022. I had never known an America without Roe. I was a post-Roe, post-Watergate, post-Vietnam baby who had been told by some dyed-hair-Hollywood-actor-jellybean-addict that ketchup was a vegetable and enriching the rich would make the poor wealthy. How many promises was America going to break? How many lies was it going to tell? How many self-induced disasters could one country create? If this is what this place had come to, then it was important to think about a post-America future.

Roe, the breakthrough that made legal abortion possible. Roe, the reproductive equality measure making us a twentieth-century nation at last, practically at the end of the twentieth century. Roe, the acknowledgement of science and medicine derived from centuries of experimentation and slow gathering of information and technique. Roe, that made modern women of us all, marking a shift in philosophy and possibility that my grandmothers had not had. Roe, the dividing line between who you wanted to know and who you thought was worthless.

She was gone. Roe, the only thing you ever got to vote on because none of the other issues you cared about, like climate change or living wages or universal healthcare, were ever things that America could accomplish. Roe, the only proof my country could do anything right by women. Certainly our paychecks could never be considered even close.

And she was struck down, just like that. Declared a witch in a trial by religion made into law and burned at the stake for being a healer. The nation I knew was officially over. And this one—no. This was one I could not respect, that had strained every bond of sanity and democracy much too far. This "new" America of ideas so old even parts of the Bible don't support the creak of the ages showing through. Well, if fire and brimstone and eternal damnation it was to be, wasn't this just the nation to bring it about? America, failing its own self-induced Gotterdammerung.

My America was over. Since it was the end of an era, I played the music marking it so—the music of my parents' generation, the generation that had been young when Roe gave life to new horizons. The only horizons I had ever known. My faithful retro boombox with the double cassette deck and three CD player with built-in AM/FM radio rotated on Don McLean, hour after hour, in one song that captured how a slice of time can die in one go. The music died, over and over, in a repeat of what had been taken, a lament of how much it meant, a world that was not the same anymore. How just one thing can be a whole movement, an entire way of life. In metaphors, when that goes down in flames, it sets your life on fire, burning the structure away and burnishing the battlements of what would come.

It had been almost impossible to cry in the years just before they murdered Roe. A pandemic in a country that celebrated the deaths of disabled people like me as we were labeled weak and superfluous, just a bit of natural selection to clear up the population and make the nation stronger. A disease not acknowledged by half of the country in a whole lifetime of being denied the medical care I needed. A body now even further disabled, still with no legal recognition of that fact despite all the proclamations of who we would include.

This place had never included me. Not in its workplaces. Not in its housing. Not in its transport. Bodies that could not be normal were never welcome anywhere, most of all in the system that said it was there to treat bodies. And now, now—an even more disabled body even more in danger for its gender. How do you make a tenth-class citizen, America, and what will you take next?

The tears were not there to spare as the Faustian bargain of right-wing power licked the asshole of an orange nightmare that had unleashed the poorly concealed and ever-lurking demons that the country claimed it had banished. False claims had become the currency of a land that had never known how to manage its currency, but I'd always had to leave the land to find those who knew that all too well.

Cry for a place that had always cried war against its own, as long as they were poor or people of color or too female to count in law? How can one feel about a place that feels its own original sins are evidence of saintly conduct? Cry for yourself, America, but the only thing I can spare is the hate you throw at me.

Tears, what were they when they had for so many years been replaced by horror? There was war in Europe again, which had not happened since my grandfathers had donned uniforms as young men. It was a war that had mattered, a war that had to be won. It was a war with a different reason than the wars more recently, from just before I was born to all our wars thereafter, which were waged mostly out of paranoia and profit-mongering. Regimes and dictators had come and gone since in many places, sometimes grown and harvested by America itself in its infinite sense of Johnny-come-lately expertise that so abused the expertise of those who had to fight them. They were rarely Senators on the front lines in my lifetime, and never Senator's sons. Were they your sons, America?

And how any nation could confuse necessary global engagement with war; they didn't always have to be one and the same, though that concept had evaded Congress multiple times over. And now here was a war in Europe that mattered in the same way as when my grandfathers wore uniforms, a war that had to be won for republics to exist, for equality to be a concept, for nations to have sovereignty instead of murderous regimes. And here is half my country, howling in favor of any dictator they could invite into the Oval, be he domestic or foreign, as long as he was orange or orange-approved.

Have you ever noticed it's always a "he"? Are men proportionally less inclined to support democracy, and if so, should we really give them a vote?

It was the right to vote, after all, as a vagina-bearing person, that my great-great-grandmothers and their sisters had finally won. Suffragettes who had newspaper articles written about them, they'd made such a regional name in the movement. Then again, they'd been related to the very judges whose local gavels would be weighing in on the growing regional movements for women's voting rights, before it reached the national weigh-in.

There was no kind of American controversy we could stay away from, I guess. We always landed wrong for the right-wing to think we were right about anything. Because rights aren't what the right-wing likes when someone's rights besides theirs are at stake. And America never could drive a stake through the heart of those eternal vampires. And now I guess, we'd continue to have the life sucked out of us by a bunch of bloodthirsty parasites feeding off wombs but denying them a choice, a vote, under law. Legal will never mean ethical. America hasn't gotten there yet, either.

It was difficult to feel anything but the pain of going backward into eras that deserved no such revival, yet tears still were absent as the light faded and a legend sang on, of legendary times and people, in a controversial and cataclysmic era that remade a nation and yet made nothing different for very long. We had not learned the lessons of Vietnam. Watergate was a warm-up act. And Roe was buried by the roadside in some shallow pit. As for the dead music, well—it might be the one thing that never died, that remained a message relevant and real for every era. Because we could not put the worst behind us, we could not demonstrate either compassion or connection, we just kept ending everything in an endless cycle of what we would have to fight for that we already fought about.

I don't know when it all went dark. I forget the hour I faded, sinking into a bed left behind by the last occupants, surrounded by furniture not my own in a place that was not home and now never could be. The retrotastic acoustic machine of decades past was still clicking when I stumbled in a fog across the concrete floors when the sun had interrupted the usual American nightmares of sleep trapped in survival mode.

But nothing had survived anyway, including me. I was as dead as Roe, and many times over. I knew my country would never care about me, but assassinate *her*? What had she ever offered but the freedom you all said you loved so much?

Roe was dead. I was the living dead. America was some zombie nation that would somehow manage to give even zombie corporations a bad name, mostly by being unrecognizable in any difference from a zombie corporation. It was surely time to serve some of that back with the same vengeance it had been thrown with.

Whatever happened to good old-fashioned liberal rage? When did we become holier-than-thou saints? If I was such a bitch for wanting the same rights my brother could have, the same types of jobs or paychecks or healthcare or homes that he could have by just breathing, then it was time to cut a bitch. And America, that bitch would be you.

Roe is dead. Long live Roe. But you, America—you can be short-lived, if need be. After all, needs must when the devil rides, and I don't know a worse devil than you.

Chapter Two

Lungfish

Poem: What Are We Worth?

Draw me the shape of a country that matters, draw me the shape of a country that cares, draw me the shape of any old place that views my rights as theirs.

Outline the turns of compassion, and sketch in empathy. Color within or outside the lines—just please, don't forget me.

Don't forget the frail, the silenced, and the lost—surely we're part of this country, too, though you insist we're not.

Include the broke and the broken, the beaten and the starved, those raped and robbed and left to die, forever mocked and scarred.

Build me a country on dreams, but only if you can remember...that dreams belong to me, too, you know, though you've crushed every one in quick order.

Build me a nation of options, even for people like me—defective from birth and a source of mirth for all to mock when they see.

Can I be a part of this country?

For even just one try?

When all my tries end in disaster, then you were never mine.

So I build alone and wasted, no way to simply survive.

I will exist in your wasteland.

Ignored, destroyed, denied.

Perhaps I'll build my own country.

Population one.

For I exist in your nowhere.

"For all", you've never done.

***

Story: The Already-Born Woman

Can someone tell me what in the flying lizard brains this brand-new head-twist of "pre-born" is supposed to be about? I'm a voter, taxpayer. The "pre-born" don't sound like they do those things, because they sound like they don't exist yet. It's not even saying "fetus". Like, yeah, it's not even that. It's categorized as if I'm supposed to lose my reproductive rights over someone else's passing thought of maybe having a kid one day? The passing thought is a real person to you, but I can't be.

Let me make sure I understand this particularly Machiavellian manner of defining a "person". Someone who might exist one day, is that correct? Someone who has not made it into the "already born" category? So, the already born don't get choices, but the "pre-born" determine the laws the "already born" have to live under.

That sounds like putting the cart before the horse, then calling the cart a "pre-horse". It could be me, but I'm thinking that an object before or after the horse is still not the horse. Yet I'm supposed to be a workhorse for whatever gets put before me, me being the one doing the actual pulling. As in, I'm doing the actual job to get anything to the next step and move this whole situation along.

Then again, given what the job market is like for people with disabilities, I wouldn't be surprised to see the "pre-born" on the payrolls before you hired someone like me, just so you could turn them into a more valuable citizen than you've ever considered me. The "pre-born" getting salaries will be exactly what happens next at every conservative-run corporation in America, you watch. They'll be assigned seats in Congress even though they don't exist yet. Oh, wait, sorry—that's already happened.

Huge conglomerates will be buying up every home in the neighborhood and putting the "pre-born" on deeds, even though they don't have names yet. I have a name. I have a name that's on a lot of documents in multiple nations, actually. You can check me out in so many ways. Yet there's no home for someone who is a taxpayer, voter, legally named person with a clean FBI report, who's been double-checked by multiple nations for perfectly legal and normal activities. Sure, buddy, I can see why, with my barely verifiable existence, I just don't register somehow.

Do the "pre-born" have bank accounts? Can they? I'm sure they already do in Florida and Texas. And are making whopping donations to political campaigns. It helps them get driver's licenses for cars they can't drive because they don't actually have physical form yet. Probably someone's got a whole rental fleet specifically catering to the "pre-born" driver. No need to pass the driving test, or even have a credit card, because the pro-life movement has already paid off multiple high-ranking officials determining official policy in America, or I just don't know much about how Supreme Court vacations seem to work behind the scenes? Yeah, it could be me. I might be wrong.

Have the pre-born ever helped you move or bought you a birthday gift or sat with you at the funeral home when your relative passed? Have they done your laundry lately or made you a meal?

I've noticed a lot of adult women do those things, you see, that's why I ask. It just seems to me like adult women make a lot of contributions on the personal and home front and well—did you notice that, too? Nah, it might just be me.

Or it could be that adult women do all that so well and have forever, smoothing the way for you that you didn't even notice it all humming like clockwork so you didn't notice the adult women there. After all, they never get a paycheck for that kind of work, so, there would be no way to track it. Nothing you could measure. You'd just have to pay attention, but chances are, if there isn't something financial you can get out of it or that you have to put into it, it's just not something your elected officials are going to measure. Because societal measures are so amorphous, so wishy-washy, and campaigns are made of cold, hard cash. Which means that is what your government is made of, too.

That makes me wonder whether the "pre-born" are like Jason Bourne, existing yet not, ninja-slicing their way through the shadows with multiple passports and Swiss bank accounts. Heck, if you've ever read the Pandora Papers, you know it's all possible, so...just realize sometimes the absurd is literally what the rich and powerful are up to before vast networks of journalists catch them dead to rights while governments of the world complain they just can't find the information the journalists keep finding all the time.

In a world where fact is fiction and what should be fictional, due to how offensive it all is, can be made into fact every time if there are enough bad actors in play, there is always the off chance that something very much smelling like horseshit is happening. There may even be pre-Bourne pre-born out there somewhere. We'll see if that bears fruit or fruitcakes, you just never know.

Do you think the Post Office will be forced to offer a "pre-born" stamp? I prefer birds, but America is full of birdbrains and Congress loves shoving the Post Office around, so, we'll see. Sometimes Presidents and Congresses like stacking the deck against the Post Office, too, a public service specified in our Constitution that's been forced to privatize. I'm not keen on auctioning off pieces of our founding documents, but everything's for sale, I guess. And every one.

What should the "pre-born" stamp look like? I'm thinking a Jackson Pollack painting, but you're probably thinking hearts and flowers. You're nicer than I am, and you probably have a job and healthcare that I could only dream of, so fuck your stupid flowers, this is my book.

Maybe it should just be a rusty hanger, or a still from the streaming series of *The Handmaid's Tale*. But I guess those options are so cliché and so expected, we should really do something surprising. Maybe a platypus. Let's just make it hybrid and unfathomable, an egg-laying mammal from a land far away. I think it kind of sums up, in a metaphorical way, our current state with women's reproductive rights in America. Yes. A platypus it is, just to make this unthinkable patchwork more palatable somehow. It's much harder to hate a platypus than it is to hate the Dobbs decision.

Here's the thing: the "pre-born" will not always thank you for fighting for their theoretical existence if they do ever get born,

America. Not everyone thinks being alive is the most important thing. Not everyone wants to be.

You see, some of us "already born" consider *quality* of life to be the most important thing. And we just don't see how that can be provided if the only measure is "barely almost maybe alive wait for the update we're not sure yet". Some of us "already born" have questions about that as a definition of either life or the value of it. Especially when the "already born" get canceled out of all conversations unless we're waging war against the "already born" so that the "pre-born" can have more rights than we're currently allowed. Some of us "already born" think because we definitely exist, and have driver's licenses associated with the actual body we use, while we vote and pay taxes, that we should have more say than the "pre-born", not less.

The stupid thing you do is assume that means we are all against the "pre-born". But if I know anything about you, America, I do know what a dumbass you can be. Actually, we just think that because the "pre-born" will eventually have to occupy the wombs we walk around with, we're gonna need to have some say in how that works.

We are the only way they can get born. They have to go through us. We're the highway, the gatekeeper, the only home you've got for that particular state of being. It's like preventing a maintenance crew from working on a road—wtf kind of result do you think you're going to get if you prevent all maintenance and repair from happening? That's going to be one shitty road to drive and a lot of accidents could happen. Fatalities, even. You should know that,

America, because it took you fifty years before you realized you needed to invest in your infrastructure after apparently assuming all infrastructure self-repairs with AI bots or something? Seriously, wtf were you thinking? Do you honestly not understand potholes don't auto-fill just because you tried to manifest road fairies?

Yeah, that's about what the "pre-born" seem like to me. Magical manifested road repair fairies that take some type of mentality disconnected from reality to believe actually exist. We're told to think of these theoretical beings as gods that should dominate our lives as we offer unto them whatever "already born" sacrifice is demanded.

Well, I suppose empires and terrorists have demanded similar things in their holy wars for gods they are just sure they speak to and for and directly with that are more right and righteous than all the other gods that have been believed in over the course of human history. You name it, wherever you look, every asshole has the answer to the great beyond all the time.

Except we're talking about my time. And my asshole lies very close to my uterus, all the better to shit on you with. You come for my uterus, what kind of crap you think you're gonna get on your hands? Don't get too close. The "pre-born" can't make it stink in here like the "already born" are capable of, you just remember that. Toilets don't self-clean successfully, either. Remember that, too, America, as the "already born" are the only ones capable of scrubbing your waste away.

***

Chapter Three

Vocal Chords

Poem: Anniversary

And where were you, all this time, to defend my life as mine?

Parts of me, surrendered, like paper autumn leaves sighing downward to a bleak Thanksgiving table.

Thanks for what?

And who has given such? Who exactly has received?

Selective deafness serves the sacrifice of women at this table over purpose-fattened flesh, tressed out for your denial.

This meal is vile

So let's go sing!

Obliterated sisters, hear your song—there is a choir, millions strong.

No day holy until we bless it, no holiday until we feast.

If we are half the sky, then we unleash!

And if half the world should drown, maybe that's better than what we got now.

After all, who is the world after? After all, we have been wronged.

And the female half ain't half been heard from yet.

Just nine black robes in Biblical apocalypse, only capable of bloodshed.

Tell me do they speak for you?

What judge, what jury, what court, what paper will induce a sequence of events that opens caverns to fall to our deaths?

If death is what you want, we can deliver while you deliberate, declaring our bodies owned by the state.

Oh, truly, fools all, what is this really about?

They should have no rights at all, forfeiting their humanity, passing over our sanity, acting as if some tome of vicious ancients should ever be debating what there's no debate about—

legal, illegal, safe or danger, priced to gouge—

whatever, you mercenaries—we'll figure it out.

***

Story: Speech or Money; Same BS, Honey

To say that I was upset at the Dobbs decision would be the type of polite understatement I'd be expected to make. Being female, I'm not allowed to be angry, threatening, or violent. Hell, being female I'm not even allowed to use declarative statements, unless it's about a make-up product.

Like, you know? It seems to be something we're not allowed to do? All straightforward sentences have to be posed as questions or we're being too aggressive? Yet if a guy said the same thing he'd be seen as decisive or funny or insightful? And plenty of women are narrow-minded enough to buy into this and brutalize other women with it, too? And pretty much all employers in America? Mmm-hmm. Bite me.

At this point, I feel as if I'd rather be burning entire cities to the ground than be told one more time that "it's about the way you say it". No, it isn't. It's about the fact that women speak at all in ways that make you feel uncomfortable. About subjects that ask you to face things you don't have the guts to admit are real or valid. America, you have never let us speak for ourselves in the tone or language we would actually use.

For example: hey, United States, I think you're a misogynist fuckup for taking away my right to choose. See how I was neither nurturing nor supportive there? Did you notice I did not pose my declarative statement as a question to gain your acceptance or beg for the right to express my anger while trying to avoid being fired or killed for having that anger? I just basically told you I think you are an inexcusable failure as a nation. I meant it.

Now, look at this acrobatic and much-maligned, completely unacceptable follow-up: Also, I'd like some healthcare and paycheck, ever, you lying sack of shit so-called "land of opportunity". See how women actually think and express themselves when they have nothing left to live for and are really digging down deep beyond your trenches of "if you just smiled more"? Great, I'm so glad we're all absorbing our I-don't-have-any-power point presentation today!

Real-world case in point of speechifying problems we're all having here: the reactions to the *Barbie* movie. So many women recognized the same language and attitudes they'd been dealing with their whole lives. But could only wear pink and talk with each other about it. So many men melted like the Wicked Witch of the West in some incoherent rant over how stupid, irrelevant, and hateful the movie was.

Wow. I'm personally embarrassed for all of us here in America. If all it takes is one movie to produce a mushroom cloud of gendered nuclear response, gee, do you think it touched a nerve? Do you think we honestly have the strength or maturity as a nation to discuss...well, anything? Especially by god if women are involved!

I'm tired of your "speech demands". Clearly women get different rules and responses about it all. I open my laptop and some bizarre past-present-future mash-up of Victorian freaking England is there to greet me with a GOP corset while screaming at me to be a girl boss.

Now, speaking of that Dickensian laptop, when it comes to how people communicate, America, some notes before we continue. You don't even have the same laws your allies do about data privacy and security. GDPR is one example, I do hope you look it up. In stark contrast, we're not making much progress in comparison to our so-called "comparison countries" when it comes to the ownership, profiteering, and abysmal mismanagement of your identity. Ever tried to "opt out"? Had any robocalls lately? Subscribe to a service that alerts you to possible identity theft? You'll need it, because we won't legislate like our allies do. Nothing about you belongs to you here, American.

The U.S. also fails to measure up to many of our allies' legal standards on libel and defamation. What can be said about whom needs, apparently, no factual basis. It also cannot include any vocabulary or punctuation you'd expect of a fifth grader doing a book report. Kids in a classroom are held to higher standards of proof and discourse than the adults around them, which makes for a freewheeling and costly competition where those who have genuinely been wronged have nothing to fall back on but begging, spending, and long years of torture.

Do you realize how much of our American content must be removed or rewritten entirely when it crosses an international border? Even self-published authors must know these things. My god, why doesn't Congress?

And speaking of Congress, then there's hate speech and misinformation. And how much exposure—I'm sorry, recruiting, no wait, I mean bullying of minors—hang on, I'll get this...no, no, it's all "free speech" here, isn't it? It's not as if multiple Congressional hearings about social media companies over multiple decades that have still produced zero meaningful change might be another example of our refusal to set limits on the quality, type, or legal status of communication in this nation. Just call everything an opinion and let the chips fall where they may!

Meanwhile, we're expected to worship and revolve around being digitally connected on every screen there is, more than we ever have been. That is a dictate, to see that as progress. Heresy to question it. But all there is, because of all we allow, are the consequences of endless permission slips always given to dangerous types of communication, information, and disinformation. And the people and organizations behind them.

Judging by the timelines and results, it does seem like the law lets the rich and vicious vomit bombastic bullshit for eons before any accountability can be forced. Those who are being slandered and hunted have the burden to assemble their own forces and resources for an interminable fight when you draw the legal lines so wavy, so fuzzy, so pricey, that anyone with enough viral hate power and funding can drown out the place where you ought to have drawn the line, decades ago.

So, America, instead of any boundaries that might limit ownership of your identity or hate made into actionable death, instead of clearly defined and consistently enforced standards of fact, proof, and indeed even passing fifth grade, what you have is an entire digisphere warring over what might be true, who might be real, what could be done but never is, and other delightful clusterfucks.

Those are just a few notes to keep in mind about our speech, our identities, and the entities involved.

Then there is the shallow end, and a lot of daily gendered expectations and insults sit there. I mean, c'mon, how many times has the feed been freaking out over whether plastic surgery is acceptable, done well, or needs to be a reason why any given influencer should be your god or be burned at the stake? How often does apparently absolutely everyone decide whether a woman, be it a neighbor or a celebrity, have your all-important permission to be employed at what job based on her height, weight, and youthful look? Yeah, H.R., you fucking do that, too. Yeah, America, that's you. When it comes to how this country talks about women, and what women are allowed to say, and how they should say it according to you...shit. I know I constantly feel like I'm DM'ing the Jurassic.

With your lax legal and systemic standards and mentalities of eras past that never passed the ERA, if you can't keep all your old forms of herd-bound outdated nonsense, you can certainly invent new ones, on technologies that have made you into the product while you try to out-perform people you've never met in an escalating war that always involves gender. Modern technology meets rotten minds stuffed full of ancient stereotypes of what anatomy has your freaking permission to exist, and at what level. While having a legal system about that famous touch-of-a-rage-at-a-button instant-click so-called "discussion" that resembles...no legal system about it at all. Nice work!

It is a miracle that I speak to any of you at all. God knows I wish I didn't have to. From death mongers to outdated shitkeepers, you've really done a number on yourselves with the quality of your standards and interactions.

Yeah, who is talking *with* whom about what? There's a whole lot of talking, a whole lot of whom, and zero "with". You don't just have the hate groups to deal with, or the tech twats to finally slap some laws on; it goes into every walk of life. We're unprotected at essential levels of fact, identity, and literacy while we're lectured about the privilege of being in isolated in gendered containment units of stale definitions remade into our daily reality via malicious SOBs and out-of-control algorithms here in the self-styled "land of the free"? No wonder we all listen so well and truly understand one another.

It's not just gender-based. It's not just the abomination America has made of its digital prowess. And it's not just the combination of the two together. We can do this about anything, everything, because we're not getting to the main point, ever. The main point awaits you later, but first I have more speech you'll hate so I can put it into this book you think I shouldn't write before I let you even understand the connections. Okay, let's deal with some more examples of crap boundaries and social ostracism in speech and public presence that you'll frequently find in what jokingly passes for a public square of "dialogue".

Anyone in this culture of toxic positivity who has the brass to tell you that you can stick your false sunshine where the sun don't shine and grow a spine that can handle the burden of talking about problems and working on solutions; that's an outcast. A heretic. Anyone who even hints that perhaps you can stick your flavor-of-the-month psychopop in some forgotten file because it's hard to see solutions in mob-fueled emotions-preaching, especially given the sky-high suicide rate in America that relates to many *economic* factors, is just someone who doesn't understand.

Really? The staggering cowardice of those who demand to be told that everything is fine when by the numbers one can prove it is not, are the enablers of people and systems that already aren't working out well. I want to know what quasi-religious therapy-du-jour on the internet has provided exactly how many job, housing, and medical solutions for whom? Um, dude. The people selling it to you.

God forbid the practical intervene on your self-styled mythology. Speech after speech describing a country I can't recognize, as I'm told it's my attitude and not your trash people and systems who might be a problem. But what if the problems are real, anyway? And beyond one individual?

I haven't noticed either our workplaces or the therapists or the influencers or the legal system appreciating economic stress, nor solving it. We just have mental "homework" and bills, or we're forced out of participating at all, here in a nation where "work" and "homelessness" can equally exist in someone's life and all medical care is just dollar signs for special interests, celebrities, and online entrepreneurs.

Meanwhile, Congress ignores poverty rates crafted by the very legislation they helped to pass to enrich the already rich, while also never telling the special interests in charge of our so-called "medical system" that finally, they've been cancelled. While the unemployment rate for the worthless, dumbass bitches like me who you've always hated for our birth defects and medical problems, we the disabled so unworthy to be considered "we the people", are stuck for decades around a seventy-five per cent unemployment rate. Get to know those Department of Labor statistics. Not that you've ever cared, but I'm one of them.

So, clearly, absolutely no one is under so much economic stress that they'd *need* some type of trained, qualified therapy while never being able to access or afford any of it. While their economic and health situation gets so bad they feel the only thing they can do is end it all. Then, then, you top that off, you abusive, evil, arrogant, ignorant nightmare of a nation, by taking away my right to choose.

Now that the country is talking about mental health more, have you ever looked into some of the main reasons researchers have found about why people think about suicide? You will always find money is one of the top-cited factors. What are we doing about money, work, healthcare, housing, transport as a *solution* to your appallingly-named "mental health" stigmas you sling? No, you can't understand that it way, can you? So we'll just put up with revenue-generating emotionbabble sales pitches from profiteering internet hacks.

And here's something that's an insult to add to it; a gendered stereotype about that economic stress and mental health connection. Your country will tell you that only men think of ending it all when they lose a job, a business, struggle economically for too long.

Our society will tell you with a straight face that women never think about it that way.

Oh, this woman has. Still does. The lifelong insult of not being considered worth any paycheck at everything I have done and can do? The inability to provide for myself as a medically disabled person while I'm billed more than your house cost to try to save my own life? Decades of that crap? Yeah, mofos, money is always a reason why, male or female. I mean, you know that, don't you? Shouldn't you? Shouldn't our lawmakers?!

If, in reality, money concerns unite us across gender lines, how come we can never see it that way? It may be my wild imagination, but I would think both men and women could talk about money as if there are many deep mental and emotional stressors that deplete us of all dignity and fight, leave us out of the loop, let us fall, and fall, and keep falling here in a country that is clearly failing the average worker...and that so much of that involves whether we're going to make it another day economically or not.

And women's paychecks lag. Their investing, their C-Suite presence, hell, their presence as judges in the system that judges us all. Since it takes having that top job, that societally-defined mark of "title that must be listened to because it gets to say what happens next", well. With women in fewer positions like that, how do we get heard or seen? What can we make happen if we don't have the title that gets to decide? And if our lesser amounts of money don't impress a class-based, wealth-stratified society, how much literal financial ownership have women amassed to be "permitted" to show up, shake it up, and make you listen?

Well, yes. Yes, that's the law. It's also the way the pay-to-play internet works. Legal or financial, the right to be heard or seen, the ability to make that happen; it's all money. That's already been decided by the Supreme Court, the equivalence of speech and money.

The big businesses did not object, because here's the follow-through for a one-two punch of what we'll have to trace down the poisoned path. The Supreme Court also decided on the human nature of a corporation, clearly just like an individual person. The Supreme Court took away our three-dimensional humanity and handed it to companies years ago. We're now the same as an entity on paper. All people here. People, paper, entities, dollar signs. If you cross enough lines, you can blur them all together.

Meanwhile, every court in America is doing jack shit about telling these people—I mean, corporations—I mean, people—that other people's identities like yours or mine are not products, and cannot be owned by anyone other than the actual physical three-dimensional person. You see what happens when you erase certain basic definitions of being a person? Product, person, entity, identity. It's just a factory assembly line.

Lines we won't cross also include these lines other allied nations have drawn, that we refuse to. Since speech is money here, buying the right to speak is not a problem for the rich. The corporations. Now, let's combine that with our lax standards of libel and defamation, our limp dick definition of hate speech (always described in America as "free speech"); it can all be purchased.

So, whatever line you want to draw to get away with whatever crime or abuse or denial you wish; all yours, for the right price. Some speech will never be seen as crime or accessory to it when there's enough money to say it isn't. Entities are people and people are paper and paper is money and money is speech. Welcome to the life-sucking spiderweb your country has crafted.

But it doesn't stop there. Why would it? The buck never stops anywhere when we can redefine it so many times. After all, the very body supposed to represent our bodies in this nation's legislation has legalized what could be seen as egregious forms of bribery and corruption. It's called "campaign finance", a merry dance in hell of how much private money can be shoved into public elections.

So yeah, I guess you better own a lot of this place to buy the ability not just to be heard or seen, but also represented in our top body of legislation. What happens if you are a poor body? What happens if you just can't own enough of it all to be a part of this place and its speech into money into Congress into law?

It follows then that if women are economically behind, we are legally behind. It also follows that since our speech, our presence publicly and privately, must be bought and paid for, how can women afford the right to speak? Since it has to be purchased, how do women gain the cash to make that transaction? How many of women's medical needs or housing crises or domestic violence situations can we afford to pay you to listen to? Because that's obviously the system.

How much cash I mean speech as me myself the not-person because I need to be a paper entity person that owns other real people's identities for money that I make off of them while I claim I can't do anything about free speech or hate speech same thing whatever because it's such a right as long as you can buy it or buy them whichever same thing…out of breath, out of cash, facing death…yes, how much money can I amass and shove down your sanity-swallowing throat to talk with you about buying my reproductive rights back? Or, actually own enough of your public presence and speech and job and company to demand it be done, because of my contribution?

Uh-huh. There's more than one Supreme Court decision that needs to be struck down before I have the right to speak. And more money than that to get beyond just speaking. I can't imagine how much money it would take me as a woman to pay my way toward being able to say what I want, how I want to, and still somehow be employed, or safe, or even a full adult under law able to make decisions about my own body.

Until then, I've got the right to bleed out on a bathroom floor at home, afraid to be put in jail for hemorrhaging from a cyst that is interpreted as a miscarriage, which you've made into a crime. Meanwhile I'll stay silent and alone, not rich enough to be healthy or cared for in an emergency while I spew hate at a system and a nation that clearly hates me, because I'm not wealthy enough to force the entry and pay the fee to be seen, heard, or believed.

Chapter Four

Archival Footage

Poem: Equation

And I have given up the fight to somehow once again take flight.

No hope delivered. Nothing yet achieved of anything that mattered of what used to be my dreams.

With maps still present, yet no course to chart, the art of living nothing like art.

And time the scavenger at the heels of what can be carried as nothing heals.

The wounds are not the gift and I will give no grateful praise,

but gather what remains of the remainder of what is left to sort and build,

cobbling together from the rubble,

expected always to be humble and step aside for you, at every
turn, (but I will not)

because you just know so much as all the bridges burn.

And I will be the one accused of setting them on fire.

But perhaps I'm just the vanguard of the nation's funeral pyre,

with half decayed and half away and half again long gone,

a country's half-life half-considered as half go stumbling on.

What's left unbalanced is left unmeasured as we are tortured
with half measures.

What equation can you add better when half say one can't
count?

America, unequal, counting millions out.

What happens if we make a road where you thought none could
be?

What happens if this half makes whole the promise to be free?

What other half would have to go to make that happen here?

What have you summed of me, my country, what do you need
to hear?

***

Story: Everyone's Got A Different Bible

I've heard so much about this bestselling book here in America, called *The Bible*. But it's like everyone's got a different one? I mean, none of the many-referenced Bibles seem to say the same thing, if you listen to what people say is in their particular version versus someone else's so...it just doesn't seem like it can possibly be the same book. Maybe just different editions. Different editors?

Have you run across this? Somehow "chapter and verse" of one person's "*The Bible*" is directly in contradiction with another person who also quotes "chapter and verse" of their "*The Bible*". Perhaps it's down to the publisher, who knows. I've got to wonder what that publisher was doing in issuing so many editions of such variety.

Maybe the editor couldn't decide on a version and just kept taking swings, probably based on whatever focus group they'd scraped together who didn't like the last version. Or, it could be that they are entirely different books from different publishers, because after all, titles can't be copyrighted. If one "*The Bible*" is the title of a DIY plumbing manual, and another "*The Bible*" is a summer garden recipe book, that could explain a lot. Let's face it, there's a whole lot of floods and "wheat from chaff" kind of anecdotes there.

I was thinking that there might have been competing publishers, with these non-copyrightable titles. It could have gotten out of hand. Let's face it, the literary world goes through its own trends and fads. If this whole *The Bible* topic was super-hot on the socials, maybe different publishers faced fierce competition in getting to tell the same material from different perspectives. Kind of like when there were two OK Corral movies in the same year about Wyatt Earp and Doc Holiday and a bunch of gunned-up drunk guys? Even after there had been plenty of OK Corral movies in the 50's or something with the same narrative, somehow the story remained fresh for re-iteration because it said something...violent or twangy or dusty or something else essential about America. Apparently. OK.

I wouldn't know, because I write what matters to me and generally ignore what everyone thinks should be copycatted. Then I copyright it. I'm a bad person to ask about all this, because most of what I've read and everything I've written is not *The Bible*. I just know that book is used so frequently about so many things, it's hard to believe you couldn't fill entire libraries with every single version of only that one title.

Some people say this one book ought to be the basis for every single law book, too. I wonder where the Bar Association is on that issue? You know lawyers will have plenty of opinions and stuff their own libraries with them.

Anyway, these people who say *The Bible* is actually a law book want that "*The Bible*" book stuck in every law library and also stuck in every law, so much so that they say they will make a law making sure their "*The Bible*" is the only law because their "*The Bible*" says it should be the only basis for law. I've heard that called "circuitous logic", but I can't find any logic in it whatsoever. The "*The Bible*" law people tell me that their *"The Bible"* is the only law book ever written or ever needed, but then I wonder if they have heard of this other document called *"The Constitution"*, which I am told is also a law document. And that it even has amendments which are also valid law documents. Like, for a whole country.

But see, here it turns out I'm backwards and sideways again, because it turns out everyone's got a different *"The Constitution"*, too. I guess the idea is to bat them all back and forth like ping pong and just see if anyone can hit them or where they all land. It's less like a library and more like a sporting event, they tell me.

Some people say it's like walking through a modern art museum with different guides and if you do it enough times, you feel like you've been to fifteen different museums even though it's the same exact place. That stark blue square might be a commentary on post-war living conditions in a time of widespread starvation, or it might be the latest weather report. It all depends on *The Constitution,* and which version you've got in your hands to play hacky sack on the quad with. It's weird how it's always people with museums and quads and paddles who are able to join the teams and play *"The Constitution"* sport. I hear the tailgate version is drastically different and usually involves exploding beer cans. I've heard reports that it's a law that *The Constitution* is everyone's national hobby, but I'm bound to wonder whether that law is from *The Constitution* or *The Bible*, given all the competition with those books to be law.

When I proposed a Monster Trucks rally-to-the-death match to decide the issue, I was soundly rebuffed. I was told I didn't understand a thing about any of it. So then I said "chess" and was booed out of the forum. It's just that it's awfully hard to understand where all these books that make all these laws are coming from and how they can exist together when a country's playing ping pong with invisible divine beings while saying these old dudes with feather pens are actually the gods of laws. What I've noticed is everyone involved in either of those books is pretty much dead by now, so I can't figure out what the living people are up to with a bunch of dead people deciding everything for them all the time.

Now see, then I thought, wait a minute…what if they aren't books or sports or laws or art or anything like that and everyone's just been having me on? What if it's like email addresses, and everyone's got their own email address at a bunch of different email providers? You sign up for one of the services, choose your moniker, like BibleExpert@herewegoagain.com or Constitution Dude@you'llneverhavemyjob.gov, and hit send. I mean, if this was email, it might make more sense as to how this all plays out and what everyone's working with here.

It could be just different social media platforms, too, right? What if there's no real *"The Bible"* or *"The Constitution"*? What if it turns out they're just internet memes?! And people make lots of comments and jokes and the meme goes on and on and on forever, like "Florida Man". It started as an observation in a news story, then became a joke, then somehow everyone had been so exposed over so many years they started imitating it and it became a way of life that was never, never, never supposed to get so much attention or StupidCon fan stan worship. They should just remember that their "*The Bible*" tells them that worship is reserved for their God and not Florida Man. Or apparently their "*the Devil*" might get them. But they get a "get out of thought free" pass because their "*the Jesus*" will forgive them. However, I sure never will.

Yes, for widely available and endlessly discussed literary fare, or whatever it turns out they are, *The Bible* and *The Constitution* continue to make word waves coast-to-coast. I should ask Book-Tok, but I'd need more than a five-nanosecond video to absorb the information they could provide, because it takes light longer to travel to my retinas than the time most of the videos last. But I bet the kids would know, you know? It seems that everyone's just got to get their hands on their favorite version, but with all the cornucopia and endless supply, it's a wonder those kids can sort heads or tails about it.

I mean, these books or memes or "reply all" emails of *The Bible* and *The Constitution* sure are complex and contradictory in how many versions are out there to invent new rules and sports and laws and hobbies, yet seemingly never be allowed to invent anything new at all what with all the dead people who have to have a say in it. Still, it seems that as usual, I'm likely missing the point and remain very out-of-touch. I'll have to see if I can get the old *Clifs Notes* versions off of eBay before the big exam coming up in 2024. So far when I've requested copies I've just been told I'm a very nasty woman.

Chapter Five
Pilgrimage

Poem: Nightlight

Stars beyond and stars within but where does your "in" lie?
    And who has room, and for what reason, for bitter is the night.
    Travelers come and travelers go, and time is hard to reckon.
    So many roads go past this place, the doors will close and open.
    Some are there that see the wisdom, using light of day.
    Whatever star, always a map, to point to many ways,
    for many worlds to still remain under many stars, for many paths
for many travelers,
    no matter "theirs" or "ours".
    The day-star always used by all, for each and every reason,
    the day-star is the life itself of all the growing seasons.

Wildflowers and harvest, all must strive for the day-star's hand
at work,
    but in the stars of night, the mind of man still lurks,
    of which star and which light will shine, of who gets what in
"you" or "mine",
    of which wayfarers have the way and who will see the light of
day,
    as if days last forever.

***

Story: The Three Wise Men

There once was a man in uniform, who was the son of a preacher. He had grown up migrating in a Model T around the American West, familiar with spice and Spanish and the gold of sunsets across wide skies. When the warp of the world threatened those skies, he went to war as so many did, taking to the skies he had once seen from the ground in the service branch assigned to fly.

But this man, young then, had flight of a different kind. His mind had always amazed, and over dirt roads and missionary barrels, whatever schoolhouse he'd land in next could simply not contain him. Many books took hold, the same way many perspectives did, mirroring the many towns that had been home, for a while. While his father warned of fire and brimstone, the church could not stop how the world had changed, nor what world of languages, cities, foods, and young pathways of substantial travels had already taken root. And what one could take on the road, in new places always with new people; that was whatever one could carry. There was always more that could be carried within the mind than in that Model T.

Like his father, this man became a preacher, but more than that, ministered. There was much of it needed as young men died and countries reeled under what felt like the end of the world. His service was not just military, but sought the human soul. Fire and brimstone had already happened; what could be tended beyond that became this man's concern. The loss, the chaos, the smoke and ash of cities and people struck down in hatred; surely the divine could offer more than a threat, more than a punishment, more than a set of rules that clearly had already been broken.

And so a mind of migrations and church that carried books within, a mind that had seen war and felt punishment enough was already present, became tuned to a less blunt method of assessment when it concerned the divine, the human, and where or how the two could meet.

It turned out those types of minds often moved in overlapping circles. You see, decades later, he would meet a man whose family's fortunes had been drastically changed by that war, by an island split in two that became synonymous with the type of hellfire humans wielded on one another in the name of the divine, over which system of God, administered by humans, would claim the space. This man whose family had fled a fractured island had also lived a life of many languages and foods, the natural intersection of people from many places. Or, sometimes the same physical place, with eternal disagreements over languages, foods, and the god that demanded such wrath from mortals toward one another.

This younger man of the heritage of split islands, he, too, had taken all the books to heart and knew arcs of history. A heritage of generations in one place often leaves one inheriting both sides of supposedly separate peoples. So when a final division comes, one has no country then, being part of both. And despite the promises his family's new country had made, he had still grown up in the shadows of the old one. The shadows were still echoing on the world stage, unsolved in many ways, as was seen on the nightly news. And like the Model T man of the skies, he believed there could be some way besides waging death over the divine. Some way besides war and relocations, belonging only to new places because too much blending of thousands of years of heritage was too much for the people of the old place to accept.

He believed there needed to be some better way, if death at the scale of permanent rearrangements of nations was to be the result of all the arguments. The divine held appeal, but only with the knowledge of history, nations, and the constant crossing of cultures personally and politically that was the inheritance of millions, truly, all around the world. This man, too, had questions and ideas of where and how they all should meet.

For this man, it also met in ministry, as with the perspective of the man who had ministered in war. They both believed the world and God could proceed with a great deal less human-caused death over God fights. For they saw God from a multibook lens, and from the after-effects of world conflicts. They saw God from the perspective of the tuberculosis one had been scarred by when there had been no cure, and from the polio vaccine that the other had held his breath for as a child afraid to end life in an iron lung. The modern world was with them, too, and they had no need for separation. Too much had been too divided already.

These types of minds in their overlapping circles circled a third man, and paths crossed again. This third man had had doubts about the war of his generation, in which few had served, and mostly those poor and drafted. But some of his college friends had stayed their education to sign up, while others had opted out, as they were allowed to if they were university types. He wasn't sure who was right or who was wrong when all of it just felt wrong from start to finish. He had questions about his country's method of deciding things. Something had gone wrong along the way.

When he was young, and like the man of the split island, grateful for the polio vaccine so he could rejoin kid society in some normal way again, his country seemed to be on the verge of great changes, marvelous miracles in ways of living. But that living had turned divided in protest, with much-admired men gunned down in hate as a movement of generations pressed for rights that always should have been theirs. Men of faith and peace were stolen by old lies. Men who could have led countries, some who came from the church and some born of scions of society, back when even scions had to serve in war, too; they just kept being taken. The scale of what was lost could never be measured. And then a president turned out to be a crook, which gave great faith in journalists but less in politicians. It did wonders for the knife's edge sense of humor this man developed as a young person, but it's a wonder he ever joined the church.

But join he did, well aware of how unusual it was for a man who might end up a doctor or a lawyer or a CEO to consciously choose the path of the church. There wouldn't have been too many barriers there for him in secular society, coming from a more standardized middle-class life at a time of wages matching life expenses for the white middle class segments on the move for jobs and housing and healthcare and education and so on.

He seemed far less destined than the other two men for ministry, but minister he did, at a time when he saw sick people being cast out of their communities because of a dread new disease. One that was always fatal, at that time. There was, in fact, a different president now busy ignoring it. So the third man opened his church doors to all that needed a friend, a community, a place to be treated as a human being. And he told his congregation about God, and a son he sent, who would have done the same exact thing. He told them it was now their chance, to rise above the fear, to embrace all the facts that could be gathered, to do unto others and live in the way of the one they came to worship every Sunday. Most of his congregation chose to stay, and to welcome those from miles away who others had condemned.

The Model T man of the skies who had been scarred by tuberculosis when there was no cure and the man of divided island heritage who had been happy for his polio vaccine; they were doing the same, at the same time, to stay the panic and include the excluded. All three men were united in their commitment to do as they would have needed someone to do for them. All three men were not afraid of universities, and two had commanded classes before, one even an entire school. They believed in the loaves and fishes of facts and compassion. Science had served them all well, when it came, and they held out hope, in the dark days of god wars over what books of faith had said about disease, that human hearts could one day be the miracle that science could, too.

They lived it as their commitment to their faith when one more time their country was screaming death and human hellfire as

God's way, but they didn't see it that way. They had seen God in the spicy food they had shared while learning a new language. They had seen God in the giant cities and small towns, where schools and libraries had been sanctuaries just as sacred as church to those constantly on the move. They had seen God in the science that saved their childhood friends. They had seen God in truth uncovered, in legal rights that tried to right wrongs, in bodies politic who had long been denied the right to their bodies. They had even seen God in doubt, and were not scared to meet him there.

These three wise men, or perhaps they were three shepherds (for none had the fortune of kings) who all sought that star over the manger, each in their way in their own lives of similar overall minds who circled one another; they knew God moved through men. That it was men who had to choose. That it was men who had also denied others the right to choose for themselves. That while everyone was screaming about God, one could quietly live in a way that might better match the best of what had been written or said about Him.

And if all practiced faith in the ways that these men chose, I could much more admire religion. As it stands, I'm afraid I was overprivileged in my access to people of faith who lived it for others' benefit, no matter the "others" in question.

You see, I knew these men. While their faith never took with me, I've always been taken by the idea that it could be done in the ways I saw them live it. It struck me, seeing so little difference at such a young age between the best of the secular and the best of the faithful making the same efforts of education, science, and legal rights, that whether secular or faith-based, one could live like these three shepherds, who were wise men.

But wisdom is a choice that includes knowledge and compassion that has to be lived to be felt. So, whatever star you follow, what gifts do you bring? And for whom?

Chapter Six

Table For One

Poem: Prowling

Have I been asleep, afraid, or only half-awake?

In the twilight of the half-life of half-forgotten dreams that leave the sticky ghost-wisps, like spider webs, that will not shake—where have I been gone?

In the half-light of a day I only know what is gone. In the night I see horizons and the lighted worlds to come.

When you write, years after, it will always sound like an adventure.

But the desert holds the echoing pain, the woods' deep water holds the mirror to all the ache of needs that have never been.

The question is not, "will I ever live again?"

For this is a birth of a different kind—one chosen walking upright for the very first time.

This one has spine behind it and an opening of the eyes, a womb-wracked kitten battered by hunger and the sunlight.

Shades of tigers weave and fade where an alley cat now stands.

What prides lie in wait in seemingly familiar lands?

I can say, "it was my life". And the goat god Pan can laugh and work his pipes.

The reference is not lost on all the loss to come—bend down, willow, as the cypress peels and sighs, sloughing off the life of the lives behind it—the heaving swamp with its panther eyes casts out another shadow—a stillborn life is exorcised.

If I am to live with just this life, then one will be enough.

***

Story: Flip the Script

Are you a woman childless and happy to be so? Did you choose that purposefully for yourself? Is it working for you? Welcome to the club. We have to meet in secret, though, because we're obviously freaks and monsters.

Your neighbors will fear you. You might be a serial killer, after all, since there's something so wrong with either your body or your brain that they just know you will end up on *Dateline*. What kind of woman doesn't have kids? What Salem witch is this?

Your neighbors will totally, utterly, completely need to know *why* you didn't have kids. They are very concerned about what this could mean for the HOA and whether they need to issue a fine for some violation. If they can pity you, that will reassure them—oh, she *couldn't* have children. Poor, wrecked, unfulfilled woman. That's just heartbreaking. So you may want to give them that answer, even if it isn't true, or it could affect the status of your garbage cans on the corner every trash day. Because if it's the other answer—the only other one—then you are a psychopath!

Because only someone biologically incapable or mentally unstable would ever be childless. Those are your two options. In the twenty-first century, after we've already been to the moon, done heart transplants, and live on some Silicon Valley server that has more say over our own identities than we do...oh, wait. Maybe that's the problem.

For all that "progress", we are not even permitted to own ourselves, and progress is strictly technological, rather than perspective-based. The do-dads, the gadgets, the barrier-breaking knowledge and engineering—that's all fine. But thought must never evolve. Lives and choices must be defined by past generations of societal mandates. Socially, no evolution is permitted, even as we're all expected to pay for own upskilling on technology to get one more job that won't pay the bills.

And it is those bills that some purposefully childless women have calculated. It is our earning power, or lack thereof, that we are keenly aware will not even take care of ourselves, much less a child. That's especially true for those of us who are disabled or saddled with challenging chronic medical conditions. Oh, which brings up one more point. Sometimes if you have medical problems you just don't want to add a pregnancy on top of that, or a lifetime of raising someone else when you struggle physically every day to do things others take for granted. I mean, when we meet for our annual Secret Childless Ass-kicking Cunts Exhibition (also known as SCARE), we really talk numbers. (Double scare!)

At SCARE, we hold secret TED talks about what it's like to be a non-celebrity who doesn't have or want children. Except we call them BED talks, which stands for Bitches Educating Dumbasses. In these BED talks, we counsel against the latest TikTok trends we've seen some of our more desperate members fall into, like buying black market Ozempic to seem emaciated enough to be mistaken for a celebrity and therefore allowed to be publicly childless while still celebrated for being photogenic enough to be allowed to earn money. Members have complained that the "BED" label is misleading, since none of us really want to invite anyone into our beds ever again as long as we live, because that's the only form of birth control still legal in the United States. At the next SCARE, we'll do a BED talk about that.

For some reason, there's a lot of writers at SCARE every year. This one chick wrote a book about a fictional world where it was considered taboo to want children. People who wanted to have children outside of the scientifically proscribed method of reproducing the species, which was all highly regulated because of the drastic reduction in all this world's resources, were considered asocial and dangerous.

You see, in this story, it was well known in this fictional world that the chemical loads and disappearing land, the scarcity of potable water and repeated interruptions in successful food production, had rendered human reproduction into a cruel and risky scheme. Therefore, the nations of the world had taken a stance on free and safe sterilization and launched global programs, which were heralded as an astounding success in serving a significant portion of this world's population with hope for the future.

Over time, it had just gotten to be common practice to be sterilized, especially since living in close quarters and splitting what little money was left were such a frequent way of life in the stressful conundrum of a dying planet. People had to band together in ways they'd never lived or worked before, just to have shelter. Communities became more common, since frequent extreme weather events meant no one could live alone anymore, and some places were just gone. Burnt to a crisp, underwater; entire small island nations had needed to relocate to other nations. What was left to live on was awfully crowded. So, governments hailed these first volunteers, these sterilized citizens as dutiful, patriotic, and concerned societal members.

That PR push was basically a necessity, since the fundamental needs of human life were so hard to come by. Humans had pushed things to a degree that even when they dialed back, too much of The Before had been too poisonous and extreme to stop the damage from happening. Cycles had been set in motion that would take decades to calm, even with collective and exponential effort. If there was to be a long run, the runway length to that was generations. So much had to shift, and a shift in numbers that came not from cruelty but from choice was viewed as one option that might help.

And help it did. These sterilized adults could help care for others' children. They could teach, build, transport, treat, entertain, cook, clean; it turned out that having more adults without children helped better provide for the children already born. Because these adults could also help parents, not just kids. Especially living in the new communities, people breathed a sigh of relief that someone was there, someone they lived and worked around all the time. People could be known for who they were at close daily range and oversight became a given. Children were precious, being the future, and to mistreat the future was a high crime. But to miscalculate how many could be supported; oh, yes, that was a part of the equation, too. On balance, that favored those who got sterilized.

It turned out that close quarters and cooperative collectives of many from many walks of life did not give the room for as much denial and abuse as had been tolerated in The Before, when so many were separated into their own silos. That turnaround in human networks didn't take nearly as long as the environmental one; the one that was, no matter how prioritized, already spiraling.

Over time, as the conditions for human—and all other—life in this world kept deteriorating due to what had been set in motion in the ecosystems of The Before, it became a norm not to want or have one's own biological children. Only certain people even had enough health to be eligible womb-carriers, what with all the mutations due to the overwhelming load of chemicals the humans had liberally spritzed into literally everything in The Before. The thoughtless and rampant growth of past times wasn't even possible anymore; not biologically. Culture shifted accordingly, in a regretfully retroactive fashion.

Some cycles of chemicals had even disrupted DNA, you see, so scientific testing was required to assess who even had a chance of being a sperm or egg donor. And sometimes the womb-carriers, the women who had enough health, had to be separate people even from the donors. The process had all gotten very separated into segments. Testing the population at adult ages, getting the little pre-human cells from the Green Light Brigade of healthful volunteer donors, implanting the potential pre-humans into the volunteer wombs assessed for viability; it was collective because it had to be.

What started as necessity came to be seen as duty, to give properly assessed scientifically supervised care from idea through to actual born human. There were always multiple people involved. What was biologically the only option became a norm in hearts and minds as societally acceptable. Desirable, even, because there was so much scientific knowledge that helped create better health and well-being for those who would be born. It was seen as a way to give people better chances for a lifetime.

There were disappointments for individuals; some who wanted to be in the Green Light Brigade of little cell donors were not healthy enough. Some who wanted to be womb-carriers also could not. Full health was rare to come by in a world that had been through so much loss of water, land, food, with so much past poison circulating to boot. It was one of the factors that led people to live in new communities, anyway, with everyone needing so much help physically. Being alone became too exhausting, too risky, too disconnected from the remaining resources.

There was a readjustment, to be sure. The people who had been wealthy, whose isolation had been a luxurious experience; they were the most upset. No one else really cared, though. The Before Wealthy were so outnumbered eventually they had to just shut up.

Those regular working people who chose to be sterilized, though, they were pretty happy with things. All around, they seemed to fare the best and adjust the easiest. It might have been because they were used to living with twelve roommates in a studio apartment anyway. Yup, the Snip Snappers never joined the rogue bands of extremists who lived outside these new societies, insisting on reproducing with no science, no doctors, no information whatsoever for health or care. Most Snip Snappers wanted to be included in society and for many, it was the first time they were accepted or viewed in a positive light. Overall, they were excited because for most of them life improved a lot.

Yeah. This book, by this chick in her BED talk at our SCARE conference, it really flipped the script. The sterilized adults were heroes in one way, the womb-carriers were heroes in another, and the scientists were heroes in theirs, too. Only the anti-science, anti-collective rogue colonies trying to take potshots at the necessary re-organization of human communities really came off as bad guys. Most of them didn't last long, anyway. Without the larger groups and without the science, a lot of them just died off because they didn't even believe bacteria and viruses were real things. They also couldn't read any of the warning leaflets the collective colonies tried to airlift to them via cargo drops, and just burned them because, apparently, the rogue extremists thought the handouts were "Satan's diapers".

But in the new collective and cooperative societies, people were allowed to think and feel and live in new ways. Most of the old-timers who remembered The Before said they didn't miss it at all. They would get tears in their eyes when they described what they could remember. Especially when they talked about what had happened to children in The Before. Homelessness, starvation, disease, and barely any literacy. The young people, the old-timers said, were often just gunned down by the same type of people who joined the rogue extremist groups.

These old-timers in this book, they would get stars in their eyes about how the new societies, no matter the pressures, were what they always needed and what they'd always been promised. It had taken a scale of disaster to force the humans to live differently, but those old-timers, they relished the new ways. They said that despite the close quarters and strain on resources, despite all the changes and heartache of losses, they loved this new world, where children were seen as everyone's responsibility, as a group, each person having their own role to make sure these children, these future-builders, were on as strong a foundation as this world's societies could provide.

Anyway, that's the kind of thing we talk about at our secret childless woman group, books like that. And science. If you'd like to join, you can sign up, but there is an encrypted vetting process due to the underground way we have to operate for everyone's safety. Last year one of our organizers received a notice for a ten thousand dollar fine, sent by her state's governor, for being "an unnatural woman directly contravening the word of God", so we had to switch our group's address to the *Pirate Radio* boat and now exclusively broadcast from sea and meet on plastic garbage atolls while beating sharks off of whale carcasses for the event buffet line. But if that sounds like where you're at anyhow with this issue, I'm sure you'd fit right in. Welcome aboard!

Chapter Seven

Report Card

Poem: She Said

"It's kind of going to shit" she said, "this misogynist country of mine.

Where men reign supreme and women are barred from their reproductive rights."

"It's kind of going to shit" she said, "this feudal country of mine.

Where the right-wing kills, the wealthy steal, and the rest are left to cry."

"It's kind of going to shit" she said, "this delusional country of mine,

that claims to be great but is all about hate and has nothing but chaos and lies."

"I'm sick of being your servant", she said, so sick she couldn't work.

"I'm sick from fear of another year of hunger and heartbreak and hurt".

"I'm sick of being your servant", she said, as the hiring manager laughed.

"I'm sick of being unqualified, no matter what the task."

"I'm sick of being your servant", she said, as one more form timed out.

"I'm sick of the brokers and Wall Street perpetually cleaning me out."

"You constantly sneeze at my college degrees and tell me to go get another.

I hope you have debts that take everything left, so you can see what it offers."

"I'm tired of the shit from this country" she said, and so did its long-besieged allies.

"The least that this lunatic place could do is just apologize."

"I'm tired of the shit from this country" she said, as she tried to hold the balance,

far removed from the life-saving care she was promised by the science.

"I'm tired of the shit from this country" she said, "tired of it taking my time.

The time will come when the bill comes due for what really should have been mine."

"You've said that rape is a gift from God, that every con man can have the top job, that terror is tourism and not a mob. America, you're a worthless slob, and why should that be my country?"

"It's an easy country to hate, this country, and a difficult country to love.

For all it's done and left undone and how it says to wait.

They tell me to wait forever; they'll get there one day, they're just sure.

And I say that's the American lie and look for alternate shores."

***

Story: Proof of Concept

It sure seems like women and voters and these "already born" people just keep heading mostly in one direction. And yes, that's closer to the grave as we get older but that's not the direction I meant. Well-spotted for the science there, though, reader; I love it when reality gets acknowledged.

But I meant the one we've watched roll across America lately, where these women and voters and "already born" people decide in statehouse after statehouse that they still want the right to choose. You'd think after a few years of the trend just seeing an uptick, some of the naysayers might get a clue about where a large percentage of women and voters and "already born" people are headed, but man…some of those extremist mofos just keep heaving upstream, far away from the electorate against the current.

You've probably noticed. This repeated proof of concept makes no dent on heads wooden enough and hearts hard enough and heck, maybe they're just hard of hearing? I mean, could be.

What we may want to do is have a referendum on whether some of our lawmakers need to go for an auditory testing assessment. It strikes me as a kind of hearing damage directly connected some-how to brain and cardiac circuitry, so it must be very complex and quite different than most types of hearing issues. It's possible we'll have to install giant hearing aids in assemblies around the country due to the results we find. Reports from the doctors stating these dire medical conditions like "deaf to all reason" and "hard of ass";

let me tell you, it could go all down that torso and involve the entire vagus nerve. Right out that sphincter. Like I said, I think we are not dealing with a normal range of hearing issues here.

We'll also have to test their vision. Let's face it, we don't want to spend our taxpayer dollars on this, but it's clear some of leaders can't *see* the proof of concept, either. We certainly have a whole medical workup to conduct on what senses they're lacking, we can't just leave it at hearing. And, since most of the party "leaders" in question are men, well, they still have more medical and legal rights so we probably can get them to a doctor to be treated when life-threatening health issues happen.

I just don't know how large those letters on the courthouse will have to be for the vision test. Painting a three-story building with a giant "E" on the side, we'll have to move down the block and just F-P, next line, T-O-Z, next building, L-P-E-D that action, you know? It's great news for the painting services, nice increase in contracts, but wow it's crazy the American people have to do this kind of medical intervention and diagnostic testing to check on the capacities of the people they elected. I've personally known plenty of people with cataracts and glaucoma who took far more responsibility for managing their conditions than some of our vision-challenged lawmakers seem to be ready to embrace.

Here's the scary thought, though; what if it's actually a literacy problem? I mean, what if they can see but not read? It's back to the basics then, but so many once-basic books have been banned that I'm not sure what's available anymore. Hopefully the dictionary is, but it might have also been banned or burned at the stake already in many places, due to having "the devil" in it. With any luck, phonics are still fun and we can YouTube some *Schoolhouse Rock* for our sound-damaged, vision-absent leadership as we remedially re-educate them in lawmaker summer school. Just 'cause they never wanted to go to class to learn anything doesn't mean they get to hold the entire country in detention. I say we all get snacks and a nap while they have to clean up after throwing garbage all over our classrooms.

Actually, we should check on whether they ever did go to school. You can download anything from the internet, and I'm afraid it's going to be upon us to verify their academic and professional credentials, since, after all, we're the bosses interviewing them for the job. So far, I'm seeing a lot of resumes with election results that clearly point toward what types of systems engineering remains effective, and which ideas have failed the startup space. And to think we're in the startup space on an issue that none of our wealthy industrialized allies are; well, we're simply behind, America. It's going to take some ingenuity to catch up. We can't have fools with failed system after failed measure interview for the top jobs and try to pass their failed ideas onto our daily working lives.

They won't even cite their results in numbers on a resume because the numbers are so atrocious. These alphabet-absent mostly-attorneys are trying to play doctor while never having gone to medical school and being vague when it comes to the numbers that we all know from the proof-of-concept replication we've received the past few years when we've done the testing and implementation. You tell me, what kind of bullet point resume is "speaks with invisible being therefore speaks for everyone and if you disagree, shut up"? What kind of job interview am I supposed to conduct when they keep sending me hate mail saying I'm a "Salem witch Tower of Babbel slut of the darkness who needs to be boiled alive in oil", then get pissed off when I don't want to hire them? Seriously, when's the last time you did a job interview and the candidate in question demanded an exorcism to purge your office of the sin of science? You guys, I swear, I can't hire in this market! I'll just do the job myself instead.

Then again, we may be dealing with a very serious psychiatric condition. I'm no expert there, but some of these anti-proof-of-concept so-called leaders who can't hear, see, or apparently read; it's unclear whether they need to beef up on reading comprehension, go get some kind of medical qualification, or perhaps, be evaluated at whole new level of the DSM Manual for Congress. It's a very specific medical volume. Totally unfathomable, inarticulately intricate, and also banned from the Library of Congress due to the book's association with hate groups and complete neurological degeneration induced by any contact with its many chapters. Some say the book is cursed. Personally, I say it's garbage, but I can be very judgmental about the complete idiocy thrown at me every day by a nation on the edge of its own self-created cliff, so, you know, judge the source.

Except not legally. Because I'm tired of losing my rights because I'm female, so I'd prefer fewer judges and perhaps more doctors involved. But medical care, especially for women, remains more of a myth or a bankruptcy than a shared way to heal.

Apparently, some of these same exact upstream-swimming proof-of-concept deniers hacksawed their way through a bunch of lobbyists and never got sued for calling this system in question "medical" and "care", and I believe we have truth-in-advertising laws on the books, right? So now we're going to have to deal with that, too, voters, in our evaluation of these top-job seekers and their fitness-for-office results. So many lawsuits. When a system is neither a "system" nor "medical" nor "care", we're really going to have to check that product out. It may involve the FDA, CDC, NIH, OSHA, and whatever former Mad Men we can scrape together from the Ad Council to really bring the point home here.

I would also bring in the DEA myself just to get a series as amazing as *Narcos* made about the scandal, corruption, death, and money laundering involved in a bunch of gerrymandered attorneys making mincemeat out of medicine and then having the gall to charge a ransom for it. Again, my word, who is assigning what jobs to whom at this company? I mean, country. I mean, whatever apparently same.

Oh, women and voters and "already born" people, we certainly have our work cut out for us! Everything from being doctors to painters to law-as-a-second-language teachers; it's all on our plate, now. We can provide proof after proof, result after result, clear numbers and outcomes all across this country but, wow. Some people just never listen, do they?

I guess next election cycle we'll deal with the theory of gravity. It's heavy stuff, so we'll all need to brush up on our physics.

Chapter Eight

Underlined

Poem: Small Things

Blue ribs flutter under the bulb on the wire, the wire like a blacksmith-battered coat hanger after having been eaten by devils of the night

We are devils of the night, too, and they are all around us here—aliens, ghosts, the shadows of the specters that hunt the human mind.

There is a blood lust in this blood and wilted rust—a desire to die,

and a notion left untended that it could be set aright, or mended like some wall between two fields—but this is not life.

Fingers trace the ruts of barely padded bone in a room tubercular with silence and small things.

There should be rain, complaining at the window.

There should be more than mildew and desertion, more than bruises, more than planes.

The birds laugh at such misfortunes and the stars can change their place, but we are stuck—

no tears, no hope in hell, and no escape from the drumbeats on the roof above that there's no such love as country and no country here in love, that there's nothing bound for nothing on a nonstop train swimming spirals in a frenzy, blind as boulders, bent as brain.

Butcher's shop talk infringing on the sidewalk,

plenty of sleeping in the streets, plenty of praying, hobbled—the desperation of a grapefruit lost at sea.

The sky is from impressionists, but the story is of She.

I know these nights, sighing in chopped streamers of periwinkle blue and midnight grey,

Unbalanced scales and missing pennies and all.

Disowned cryptic nothings, iris vases, bonds of la guerre, la guerre, la guerre...

silence and small things are there.

But who is doing the knowing of the silence and small things?

***

Story: The Pendulum Is The Pit

Concepts revisited are never much welcome, but this one revisits itself. These metaphorical sacred cows, those tenets one is never supposed to question, those ideas assumed to be a universal truth for all time. But, the times call for some new response, don't they, since all the old ones are failing us every day?

Some say that democracy is a pendulum, swinging back and forth. Left here, right there. Oh, it's what they'll try to tell you about reproductive rights, too, since that's apparently politics and not medical science, but of course only if you are a woman. Then they also say it's religion but suffice it to say, you can see why I'm interested in what I'm told about this pendulum. Which is apparently shaped like a dick.

Yes, indeed, swinging back and forth. The dick pendulum of democracy, apparently. They say that's the nature of it and it will inevitably shift back in the other direction at some point, as if the laws of physics applied directly to human-crafted social systems in the exact same manner as with inanimate objects and body parts. I mean, obviously. Back and forth, so naturally, just a scientific law. A gravity-obeying, rule-observing state of affairs. If one thing happens, the other must follow. So predictable.

Some discuss the pendulum in slightly less robotic terms, yet still present the pendulum. A bit of a generational or world event shift and such-and-such will move that pendulum in the exact anticipated direction. Then, when new people or new things happen there will be an about-face and we'll see a one-eighty. The opposite predefined direction will be turned into. Oh-so-naturally and oh-so-inevitably, still with those universal laws.

Um, okay. Except what? What about humans and their human-made social systems follows the same exact laws of science as your third-grade science experiment? We're all just what, foaming papier mâché volcanoes where baking soda meets vinegar? Bring a tarp for the floor and Bob's your uncle, the clean-up is easy! What about the heaving sewer of the American cultural landscape can you put in a test tube and control, given the proper reagent? Because I've noticed, despite this supposed pendulum predictability, that some understanding beyond basic mechanics needs to be a given when it comes to grabby little apes with a huge mix of neurological chaos festering within.

Beyond a lack of complexity, beyond the lie of predictability, also frankly pardon me if this sacred pendulum of patronizing pedantic promises sounds like an indefinite rearranging of furniture while never, ever cleaning or repairing the house. Back and forth, here and there; who cares? Fighting over where the table really belongs in the living room, keeping it in the space of who won the argument that time around. Then doing it all all over again. And again. And again. Okay, so, there's mold in your bathroom and no lights in your kitchen, and you're going to glorify redecorating for years on end? I'm going to call that crazy and become my own contractor.

There are two poor assumptions about this sacred cow of the pendulum, maybe three. First, it assumes that democracy can be nothing other than a ping pong match. Only two sides, always playing over the same table, always playing the same game, always playing by the same rules. Are you asleep yet from the boredom of watching that paint dry? Or perhaps terrified because that's nothing like the banging you hear coming from the walls every time you turn on a faucet?

Second, it assumes that this very poor definition of table tennis democracy can and should—and it's the "should" I really object to—just reroute over the same exact pathway from the same start and endpoints into infinity. It is only two sides, evidently, and then only one pathway that is just traveled back and forth upon until the sun explodes.

And thirdly, which probably isn't important to anyone, it assumes that I am both stupid and also willing to put up with this freaking pendulum.

Fuck your pendulum. It's the pits. Notice please that I did not say "fuck democracy". I hold democracy to be too sacred for this pendulum to just push mechanical buttons about in such a repetitive and limited fashion. While somehow also creating carnage, but more so for women these days if we're talking about swinging dicks.

Seems like your pendulum is busy slaughtering what I find sacred, which is actual progress *forward*. Never needing to go over the same ground, ever again, especially if it hurt people. Building on new and helpful accomplishments instead of acting like the Las Vegas strip, demanding to dynamite one more herculean effort in the insanely overpriced and completely unnecessary quest to build something else remarkably like what was already there before in the exact same spot to then just do that all over again because we really enjoy blowing shit up.

America, for real, your democracy gets the Las Vegas strip hotel treatment and you think you've really achieved *what*, exactly?! As a former resident and fan of the state of Nevada, dude, back off. I know of what I speak and I still love the place. Don't mean I ain't gonna call you on it.

If reproductive rights in America do not reference the pendulum, I don't know what would. Back and forth. Gained and lost. Won and ruined. Oh, it's not "winner take nothing", here in the land of sporting teams brinksmanship. The winners get to do plenty of damage to those they enact their hate and violence on, or they get to spread the benefits won, but they don't ever eliminate everyone they hate.

And it also isn't "winner take all", because you never will anyway. Changing hearts and minds takes more than brute force, but we never did learn the lessons of some of our foreign forays, so I would not expect you to understand now that there lies a convincing power beyond bombs, beyond money, beyond throwing bodies at the matter. You wouldn't have encountered that anyway.

No, it's "women take nothing". It's "women won't win". It's relitigating what it is to be female, and what rights women will not have and men will, as if somehow both aren't involved in medicine and reproduction. Somehow gender and equality are beyond your sacred cow pendulum of "democracy", yet you keep insisting I am represented at the ping pong politics table of infernal back-and-forth. It's you, America, making damn well sure of continuing the gender divide with your mindless pendulum. Yes-no-yes-no-yes-no-yes-no-yes-no for women, yes-yes-whatever-you-want for men. My god, how would I spot this well-hidden discrepancy? It's not as if your pendulum is world-famous or something.

Some places pretend they are better than that pendulum, and some people genuinely are, but I know how much I've always had to fight. It took me decades to fight for a tubal ligation in your so-called "liberal" places. Oh, I will write a book about that, too. Because go fuck yourself, America, instead of always fucking me over for being female. Apparently your pendulum is not only a lie, but it's also misogyny. Roe was legal but god forbid in your supposed blue state sanctuaries of equality and compassion I could get my tubes tied.

What an odd state of affairs that was, to have the right to an abortion but not the right to prevent one. Do you see what I mean, it's a problem to be female? The pendulum swings in your favor, but only in one way, so you're still denied your rights over your reproductive anatomy. So even when they tell you about this sacred pendulum, they will always find a way to make you into the wall it hits as it swings.

Then you go, yeah, but what about the red states? Well, in my lifetime they had Roe to hide behind. The law they hated so much protected them in every way from having to do anything other than spew rhetoric and try at every local and state level to decimate all reproductive care for women. Of course, that also tends to eliminate regular anatomical care to screen for cancer and STD's, so it's a baby out with the bathwater situation.

How dare they, when enforcing as many babies as possible is what they say they value?! Oh, they tossed it all out, baby, bathwater, even the tub, because, well, that horrendous conspiracy of science that medieval Europeans everywhere are still seeking to abolish. Throwing out all that water and all those tubs, well, it did mean it was difficult to wash, but, somehow that'll all come out in the wash because everyone knows that if you just hit your version of your Bible hard enough on the issue, it will solve itself through the magic powers of invisible beings. No soap needed.

What injustice they've had to put up with, the poor beleaguered feudal conservatives, as efforts to expand care for the poor and open options for retirement-age people somehow spread like the microbial diseases the conservatives couldn't give two fucks about, except behind closed doors as they hide the fact of being vaccinated. Just look at the litany of pain the far-right has had to endure, such sinister disasters of oppressive government overreach that they rail against while cashing their Social Security checks, oh lament, lament, lament it's such a nightmare. How dare the pendulum not swing right into the necks of the people they want to decapitate? As usual, not realizing they may pull the plug on their own lives and bank accounts in the process.

Yep, it's always been an elevator-top-question mark kind of a situation with the conservatives who actually think they believe what they say. What they respond to best is hate. What they love most is the destruction of those they hate. Policy be damned, it's the demagogic personality of the biggest hater that's the really important issue about...democracy? Aided and abetted at every turn by the blinding hypocrisy of epic manipulative proportions from Ivy League conservatives who know better, but love money and the power to destroy people more than they will ever care for country. Whichever way you slice it, from the lords to the peasants, somehow my damn uterus is always involved!

If I hoisted it on this pendulum, how many people do you think I could slap in the face with it? Oh, wait, America did that for me already, how obliging. My, it does whistle nicely in the wind as it runs out of my reach on everyone else's predetermined course.

What a typical situation to now be in, to have neither the right to a tubal ligation nor the right to an abortion. What a classic American conundrum of the pendulum in its course, and the course is never set by me. It's only my body, that can never be mine. That right I do not have because I am female. That's just the same old rut whatever way you swing it, your sacred cow pendulum of democracy that never includes my decisions about my reproductive anatomy. I am female, so no wobbling dick device of supposedly so-natural and so-acceptable and so-rules-based and so-forth-and-so-on freaking trend of metaphor in what could curtail all my grown adult life choices or just my grown adult life period, swings for me. So, it's acceptable to you to go back and forth on this until the stars fall from the sky while never including me anyhow? While tying your ping pong politics to science and smacking us all around with it?

Here are my thoughts: um, no. Your same ruts ain't gonna cut it. You can shove your pendulum into the dust bin of history and try some real representation instead of metaphors made into stale animatronic combat that keep us in lockstep with the same place that got us lost before. That place that was never ours to begin with. If it all brought us here, your metronome of pendulous repetitions, then do you think there was always something amiss in allowing this sacred device to somehow always miss the point?

I guess in your ping pong two-sides sporting match of what you've called democracy and sent back and forth like a mentally unstable miniature train set burning the same length of track until the next big giant meteor meets Earth in an unfriendly way, you forgot women. The third party you've always dismissed as irrelevant, powerless, fictional. The one that's such a vote-spoiler for you to obsess over, yet speak of as an impossibility. The American people will never trust that, never see it as viable or stable or experienced enough.

Well, you may be right. That sounds like rhetoric always attached to women as much as it does to any consideration of ever having more than two sides at your power table. But in the end, your objections won't matter, because human hearts are wider than the narrow aperture of permitted pendulum pathways. There can be far more than just two ways that never go my way anyway. So swing it left, swing it right, it's my uterus and I'm gonna fight.

Chapter Nine

Advice Column

Poem: Mirage

Illusions of choice and power fade by the hour, by the gavel, by the broadcast

All men are equal but we are outcast.

In the highways of our mind heroes are we all in the starkness of our lives, but who will live to claim it?

As they all draw lines on paper that steal rivers from their beds.

What can the desert give me now?

Parched horizons in glitter waves...

Living on memories and tea, now we go, to the lost and found of some evaporating outpost,

and other strange contraptions of times past stacked in a row.

Goodbye, Roe.

Unedited yet unfinished all at once, in the raw and left to push with a shark's tooth edge for the edge of what was known, of what was so.

Sea creatures writhing on a sand dune...

Now we dance a different tune of where the wind was once—

It comes out of me unwillingly, all the knowledge that I know.

Brave as the soul allows, where is the water and how would we go?

At the lake of reeds of yesterday, we've seen the marshland fade away, to become just a harsh land now.

Tiles of ground spitting dust, boundaries so fine they cut, even the bandits abandoned us and every man became foe.

Goodbye, Roe.

A ghost town hollowed while the graveyard fills.

I know who's buried in Boot Hill.

And how many wagon tracks lead to waste under many lies of open skies—no trail, no stream, no shade.

Dilapidation as the only permitted expectation as phantom trains steam backward disappearing into past—my, how nothing lasts! And sandstorms have become the norm scratching sight into dim then blind.

But cruel is a choice as they spit roast us on their cross.

I wish it had been their Bible that they'd lost, tossed into shifting dunes as we ran to rain.

We had to run so far away. And it's only far away where the river fills now and boats are there to carry over turbulent swirls the women, the girls—the only wombs you'll ever know.

Goodbye, Roe.

***

Story: Spare Parts

What should I do with my uterus? I know that the best thing to do would be to ask a bunch of people who don't have one. You see, they've got enough distance from the issue to really assess things clearly. They're "outside the problem", so to speak, so they're very balanced third-party mediators in any uterine process. Except, a lot of them seem to want to get inside the issue, or round thereabouts, so there are times I could swear it's difficult to see them as detached and neutral about it all when they just keep demanding use of all the points of entry.

I'm not sure I really want them as mediators when all they keep doing is talking about their expertise while demanding access to all the equipment while bragging about what good problem-solvers they are while their lives never consist of living any of this anatomy. What if I demanded full legal control over their pipes? Well, I can tell you, I'm so frustrated I'd probably just be running for a chainsaw then and seeing how they liked it. I'm just not the kind of neutral, negotiating, expert third-party mediator they are, see.

Frankly, I don't intend on using my uterus, and I'm having problems finding a solution for that because it doesn't seem like a category anyone's thought of much. Whole lot of blank stares, all around, all the time. And that's just the white coats with all the stainless-steel tools that are supposed to be the licensed legal con-tractors to work on uteri! Geez, you'd think if they were experts, somehow they would have heard of just not using the thing. It's not like your heart or your kidneys or your liver; some organs, you can't help using them. There's no other option, you need some level of function there or you're just toast. Other organs, well, you don't really have to kick 'em into high gear, ever. You can live perfectly well without them, even. But when I try to tell people my uterus is like the appendix to me, then they think I've never been to school and don't know anything.

But seriously, when you type up an income and outgoing spreadsheet for the uterus, it's awfully hard to see the ROI on putting that into your portfolio. Asset prices are terribly inflated thanks to the not-crook president who took us off the gold standard, making way for some trickle-down jellybean addict to buy Congress for pennies on the dollar and create a fiat currency completely detached from all value that could be floated at insultingly low interest rates to indebt a country to massive stupidity and its inevitable demise. The kind of vehicles you can build when money is only a theory! I swear, I'll bring my jetpack and flying car to the party. It was all about that cartoony in its creation, but the revolting abuse of financial systems I suppose is not our thesis here.

And yet, think about it, that uterus and the cost of use and space these days. The cost of a fixer upper now! Don't tell me you haven't noticed! It's even worse than the housing market. Plus, just think of what could happen to the tenants. Some places have plenty of ordinances against all assistance or repairs, so how on earth can someone be a responsible landlord then? And what are the tenants supposed to do when they're just left alone with no property manager to call if something goes wrong? I mean, think about it, would you want to rent that space? Would you feel confident if you were the landlord that you could even keep it in good condition when your county told you that was against regulations? Either way, tenant or landlord, that's just bad news all around.

And whether you're a tenant or a landlord or just a homeowner, the price of it all every which way is through the roof. With the kind of expenses on insurance and repairs, you want to try being a homeowner or small-time landlord these days? It just makes everything pricey for tenants, too, you know, as all those costs get passed on. I mean, if you're at all familiar with the real estate market now then you'll know how high rents are and what housing prices are like, and the massive amount of debt we're all supposed to take on to have a space to occupy. Well, let me tell you something, the prices going on uteri these days don't seem any less! The debt can really pile up if you try to get one or use one or rent one or own one. There's nothing you can do but pay for it, apparently. And I'm just feeling shaky about the return on that investment. It's not even a good market for a flip, but I might see what I can do about some carpeting.

And what is with the mixed messaging? Have you noticed they have not sorted it out? By god, you can't take care of the space or repair it or help any occupants, but you're still supposed to make sure the space is occupied? Truly, how realistic is that? Is that the way you look after your rental or home? If it is, then you're likely just dealing with a tear-down, because that is not going to keep anything in good working order. When I pointed that out to some of these non-uteri people who did own homes they were allowed to care for, well, they did not like that much, I can tell you. They said it was not the same thing and I said they were right, because one is your health and the other is walls, floors, and roofs. Then they told me the walls, floors, and roofs were more important than health, and it proved how little I knew and how incapable I was that I could not prioritize their concerns over my own.

So I'll have to apologize of course for spreading my ignorance for thinking that there can always be other roofs, floors, and walls, but there is nothing like health to substitute for itself. I know, as a disabled person who has been denied medical care more times than I've received any, leading to increasing disability that is expected to be my death, I would know nothing about what health meant. Certainly as someone who has lived in many different walls, floors, and roofs, I would not understand how they could be rebuilt or could be shared, or could be changed. I know I just shouldn't be lecturing these wise third-party mediators who don't have a uterus about any use or repair or rights at all.

But here's the thing; if I'm by default the owner, how come I can't pull a county permit to get some work done? You have to in the real estate market for certain major structural and functional changes, and I would think that having a uterine tenant would by god come under that heading. But no. My body plumbing has fewer rights and ways to address it than my house plumbing does. But if you have a different type of body, a non-uterus body, all of your body plumbing can always be addressed properly, in addition to your house plumbing. So, I get to wondering how that isn't discrimination in plumbing rights. If we're so obsessed with real estate, then what do you call that state of affairs? Why doesn't my body plumbing count the way non-uterus body plumbing does?

You can see in all this why I've just decided to create a workaround to the issue, can't you? When my own body tissue has fewer options than a kitchen sink replacement, I just can't deal with that. I'll just sit here with some spare parts on my hands, unable to make heads or tails of it all.

I'm told I have to wait for a whole lot of voting in a whole lot of places, because we can't just have one massive vote as a whole place and be done with it. No. It's really important, apparently, to decide this county-by-county because I guess all real estate is local, right? They say that, too. But on this one I think they're lying because if a whole country has to vote county-by-county and state-by-state on plumbing then…well, it's still a whole country and it could take a whole lot less time if we did the whole country at once what with these plumbing rights.

They say at one point in time, that did happen, but it wasn't the kind of vote I'm thinking of. I've heard tell that a very small bunch of non-uterus people in baggy black dresses took a vote back somewhere before I was born in this important room that people used to admire or something like that. And if you're also saying, wait, seriously, that's how they decide these things?! Then yes, same. I know it sounds ridiculous. But maybe that's why the not-uterus people think they own the issue, you know? I guess they were allowed to then, and are still allowed to now, and that baggy black dress group is still kicking around somewhere, but I hear it's not as popular anymore. I guess it's one of those trend things, like accent walls or all-white kitchens, speaking as we are about real estate.

Mine is just going to remain unoccupied. There's too few permits I can pull, too many non-uterus people in baggy black dresses, too many places that apparently have to decide this over and over and over again because...well, whatever reason they're giving next, I know it never comes across as reasonable to me. But if anyone knows a good plumber who can keep things quiet and under-the-radar, I hear there's a huge demand for it in this expensive, unequal property market.

Chapter Ten

Uniformity

Poem: And Poppies For The Gone

For all of us, living on ill-borrowed time in a country that decided that womb and choice were crime,

We owe you hatred.

And the alliance of resistance calls to millions now, knowing they are lesser, and exactly how.

Enemies of poorly-wielded power gather diagrams to make the point of what was taken—

Oh! All men have plans.

And then we'll see who laughs the last or rises up.

Half full? Half empty? Over edge, the shattered cup.

No apologies.

Just poppies for the gone.

And what will be gone next as they say they're trying to help you as their half-constructed pretext of what text to erase.

Look at the waste of ages of rows of stones and sticks, marking what was taken and for which paper twist of who could not agree or who signed too late.

Because we're waiting for the moon, we will not draw the curtains cross to wash the room with light.

No, let her blaze blue fire and show the path through what is wrong.

There's no need now for sun when all is dim to search for bright.

Just poppies for the gone.

We can see in shadows wilted vases casting rot,

the same as generations also worthy of no thought.

Just green tables.

The sharp and clear will rise on by if we bide the time. For hunter's moons and harvest moons and blood moons acres wide.

We're waiting for those moons to show the road throughout the riddle.

Put by, store up, make do and mend, the season's coming to an end when sun can light what is not life but just a waking death.

We'll burrow underground and watch for night instead.

And no trace will be left, just poppies for the gone.

***

Story: Stars and Stripes

They gave them uniforms that resembled the flag, but long after that flag had been changed many times over. So no one recognized the pattern on the uniforms, they just knew it was of stars and stripes.

It helped with the visibility, you see. There were so many escape attempts that something had to be done to make the ones on the lam truly stand out. It hadn't worked to give them the neon colors that were easy to see. Nope. Far too often that neon resembled the same clothes worn by construction teams and joggers. There were too many arrests of people putting down tarmac and just going for some cardio. It had gotten out of hand.

But they certainly were not going to go back to the usual uniforms. Why, then they could be confused with other types of lawbreakers, and that wouldn't do. There was a priority put on these specific crimes, so the typical uniform, especially considering all the escape artists, was unacceptable. No, indeed, these offenders needed their own specialized uniforms to mark them for their particular sins. At first glance and with no doubts. After all, they were not just in for any old crime, no, these were new ones. Well, old ones, but new as well, because of the back-and-forth in the policy landscape over time.

Yes, sins the country could not abide. Ones that could only be committed by a certain group of people. Why, half the population couldn't even commit these atrocities! One had to have specialized equipment, and at least one other accomplice. And as a historic note, it should be said that for all that they debated about the best way to identify the offenders, there was nothing ever done about the accomplices, despite the necessity of their involvement in perpetrating the crime in the first place.

It has been suggested that perhaps a giant "V" marking the nether regions should be displayed in a supersized red splash. But, when that was tried, the runway really took off with the trend and fashion weeks everywhere were full of spaghetti-stick people fierce-walking their way down flash-happy platforms to critical and popular acclaim. That was not the effect the authorities had intended, and heads rolled in mass-layoffs at that uniform version.

Oh, they tried to tone it down with camouflage; the military protested and Senators blew gaskets on their ancient plumbing. There had never been so many ambulances called in one session of Congress. After that fiasco, they tried to use all-pink uniforms, but toymakers sued. What was a country to do about the extreme need to identify these prisoners properly?

White boards and stinky markers flew 'round the clock in brainstorming sessions. They zeroed in on using outdated uniforms of eras past from penitentiaries around the country. Retro yet distinctive. But the problem was clear when they all looked remarkably like costumes and escapees successfully pretended to be from barbershop quartets and baseball teams, particularly around All-American Saint's Day, which used to be some other holiday but was renamed. In general, they made a right hash of it trying to come up with a successful uniform for these very particular prisoners.

It was the snarling suggestion of a blacklisted anthropologist on trial in front of the Senate that did it, inadvertently. They'd hauled her out of some beach bar in some country no one had heard of, what with the state media takeover, and dragged her in chains to answer for her crimes. She had rather cleverly evaded being put in a uniform by altering the specialized equipment necessary to commit the crime. And the Senate felt that should indeed be its own crime in and of itself, and so she should be put in a uniform.

Because of the new state-controlled media, reports differ. The trickle-down from various Congressional aides was the only eye-witness testimony anyone had of it. That's because when the anthropologist was hauled screaming through the Capitol hallways, she spat on some very important statue of some very important guy, right on camera, then addressed the passing Speaker of the House as a "gerrymandered feudal Pope whose skills at corporate money-laundering were only outdone by his fear of vaginas", also right on camera.

The broadcast blipped off at that point, then went into *Howdy Doody* re-runs, which happened to be one of the few television series permitted under the new Christian Decency Standards, which had passed by a wide margin amidst the one-party system in place. That had been fairly easy to do, since so many millions of the other party had been exterminated in the Moral Cleansing Acts. Some said that these policies were neither Christian nor moral nor clean, what with the mass bloodshed and all, but others considered it the best sports broadcasting they'd ever seen.

So, it is understandable how only those who were physically present were the ones who could tell the tale after the cameras cut out when this woman was saying the unthinkable to the nation's Dear Leaders. It had been some time since that sort of language had been applied to anyone in office so publicly and directly on state-controlled media channels. The shock of it might not have been so shocking if they'd ever read anything she'd ever written, but writing had been labeled a subversive activity, so maybe they just were just following their own rules and not learning anything about her before making a public spectacle out of the trial of someone whose anatomy they hated enough to hunt her internationally. As you can tell from the uniforms debacle, an appreciation of consequences was not exactly the strong point of the authorities.

Yes, they say it was her words that gave rise to the present uniforms. When questioned by the Senate as to why she remained childless, and why she was not incarcerated, and why she was not sorry for it, they say she went on and on about some republic that used to exist, right where they were standing. They say she hollered to the rafters about some place where bearing a vagina was not considered an armed act of aggression. They say she gave them chapter and verse (whatever those are) about some country where miscarriage was not a felony, and made them gasp when she cited old paper books indicating this very same place had once said that terminating a pregnancy was not high treason.

No one was fool enough to believe it all, of course. She was just some silver-haired little fossilized raisin from some other time zone, or maybe planet. They knew better than she did, because their Dear Leaders' Righteous God-Given Mandates had been handed to every household, molded in the finest factory-extruded plastic and hung on walls as the Moral Authority Authorities looked on. Everyone knew those had been true for all time. At least, they were pretty sure.

Evidently it was a chaotic trial, with snorts and retorts in large quantities. But it was an offhand comment that really captured the imagination of the powers that be and led to their most successful uniform idea to date.

When accused of multiple criminal acts, some of which had not even been written into law as criminal but which the Dear Leaders knew would be and should be (which was just as good) the blacklisted anthropologist asked how many times a day they jerked themselves off with their sick version of the flag. Then she told them she hoped they were into bondage and would strangle themselves with it, not being found for weeks and having their nether regions munched on by passing peckish raccoons.

Apparently there was an uproar. But it proved to be a useful distraction for the blacklisted accused. One of the underling note-takers present that day said that while everyone was screaming and throwing furniture (which, it should be noted, was actually quite normal behavior in Congress) the anthropologist jimmied open her cuffs with a small metal T-shaped device, possibly copper, and darted between the walkers and wheelchairs of the Senators.

She snatched a cane along the way, smashing doorknobs and windows, jetting like a maniac squirrel on ledges until she could drop into the bushes.

It was a breathtaking escapade. Or, at least, the few eyewitness statements seem to indicate it. It's difficult to tell. With the ban on literacy, notes have to be taken strictly in emojis and pictograms, and the crayon diagrams differ.

What we do know is that somehow she disappeared, and six months later a Senator went ballistic on a state media broadcast about a letter he'd received in actual ink on literal paper in alphabet-made words instead of emojis. His mistake was reading it live on the broadcast. We do have that footage. The transcript is overwhelming, but the contents of the letter evidently stated, "My anatomy is not a crime, you misogynist fuckwads. If you don't want any abortions, cut off your dicks." Brief, yet poetic.

Oh, it took some time for the hullabaloo to die down. There were, naturally, some riots. Mostly in Congress. The general population was often too concerned with getting enough to eat to make much fuss. And many just didn't want to be shot on sight, since all gatherings that were not state approved had been banned, no matter their intent. That, and the fact that tanks rolled through the streets day and night to suppress any objections or discussion of the controversy in any public space meant it was truly the daring fringe and absolute criminals who would engage with the matter.

But it did get underground famous anyway, that trial. Like the telephone tree of gossip, it may have morphed many times along the way and ultimately be less than precise in its details. But it should be noted that not long afterwards, that's when the authorities changed the prison uniforms for these very special types of prisoners. That's when they wrapped them in the stars and stripes of the blacklisted anthropologist's young years.

Yes, they marked these specific prisoner women with what the anthropologist had said was the flag in her time, that time when crimes like miscarriage and tubal ligation and abortion and all sorts of the dark arts of female science had been legal. Those criminal times, when women had defied tradition and convention, thumbing their noses at the idea that they had only one purpose or could do only one thing. Those evil days when women said they should have the same rights as men. Oh, those dreadful past times.

Now, of course, so many are so grateful for the correction. At least, the ones outside of the special prisons where stars and stripes are worn are very grateful. As they are told to be, and punished if they aren't. It's truly been a remarkable solution.

Chapter Eleven

Bankruptcy

Poem: The Moon on 3rd Street

And there is nothing so much as grey-blue skies to show the contrast in her eyes

And nothing like a green-blue sea to bring the depths of what can be

Nothing like red earth to brown to show the wreck of how she drowned

Nothing like mellow clay-steamed sun to mirror back all she has done and who has done her in.

For she's six feet under yet miles away in a gamble to outrun the nation she hates,

Dripping off a high-wire act, all scant odds and little intact

She will carve what trees man made cruel and bend the bower
for reckoning,

Until it breaks. Or you do.

And simply by the wind she'll know, and fly.

Or swim.

No place to go means nothing when everything is taken.

What you see of her, you see, is only smoke and mirrors,

Your own reflection only of what stories you spin.

She is only echoes of what might have been if you were only
human,

Instead of evil, wearing skin.

And this moon by day may light the way but we still need the
third.

For the moon on 3rd street was the last time we saw the light of
the world.

It's mistake over error since that epoch,

Torn all apart.

And the soot of all wrong ways to go means black lungs, blacker
heart.

Listen wrong and all is gone, the mirror is a murder.

She's always been and never was and now, you cannot know her.

Then again, you did not want to. Then, you never did.

Pleading now for some mercy that you've never earned, but the
scythe bears her initials.

Tough shit you never learned.

And thunder sounds like ocean sounds like tunnels sounds like
rain,

And rain brings what will grow or what will wash away.

As lighting sounds like gunshot sounds like engines shocked with pain,

Confuse them all together, doesn't matter, all the same.

And all the same to you as well as what she was becomes your hell.

And hell is all that you have earned. It was that moon on 3rd street.

Hovering in thin air, pulsing luminous yet tentative, then you got argumentative.

Pack your bags, she's long bugged-out, as the bastards try to smoke her out, but brawl and boil is all she's known, so she takes that moon, and then she goes.

And you will not remember much and bets on that you'll care less.

But the contrast eyes, the grey-blue skies, the red-to-brown of battered feet on earth that she long studied.

You cannot defeat her spirit.

That is the moon on 3rd street. Her continued reappearance.

***

Story: No-Go SEO

For all your connecting, innovating, instantaneous, supposedly worldwide internet, who really gets to download the update? With women's reproductive rights, we're in the first century or we're not going to get past the mid-twentieth, apparently.

So, we're on the web but our ovaries have to live in someone else's version of what they claim as their religion made into law, then say it's not religion, yet define your entire life for you as someone else's fertilized cells that they give a remarkably religious-y sounding definition of "soul" to? It all sounds so amazingly warped and badly referenced while somehow also stunningly plagiarized that I swear AI wrote it.

I'm sorry, I must be confusing my centuries. I could swear the better comparison to what your "modern" life is here would harken back more to Medieval Europe. I mean, science also gets the axe these days, right? What with germ theory being a complete conspiracy and all, as you so clearly stated on every possible website during the pandemic.

And didn't those algorithms just love an unjust cause spewing death and stupidity by the nanosecond in geometrically expanding waves of why I'm basically freaking mortified to even exist in a context of such fossil fuel-intensive intellectual destruction. My, how far we've come!

Wouldn't a few decades in any given society show real-time shifts in the daily needs of living spaces, transportation methods, food production, and medical care? Some changes do seem to be the regular state of affairs, don't they? Certain items or methodologies fade because they don't serve a purpose anymore, while new ones may be needed. Technologies of one era don't necessarily work as efficiently, effectively, or safely as a newer version.

Things. Places. Processes. That's part of it. Unfortunately, it gets worse. What about the people?

Because no matter the advancement you claim, it's always denied to someone. No matter the achievement you say will change everything, something always feels stale about who has what access to it. Something always creeps up, eerily familiar, with every self-congratulating announcement about how revolutionary and world-altering the latest invention will be. Perhaps that's because the determined destruction of entire categories of humans via race or gender or religion or socioeconomics or incalculable quantities of dumbass still seems to be on the table, era to era.

So what can truly never be reinvented, while you claim to be so modern, so advanced, so innovative, is the human soul. What can never be budged is your belief that there's no other way than this cruelty, this stratification, this back-and-forth war of attrition that wastes lifetimes. Wastes resources. Wastes energy. And lays waste to your neurological health both as an individual and clearly, as a society. What are we really making new or better versions of here?

Is it a new and better society just because we have more or faster devices? It doesn't even feel as though we're meeting basic definitions of a society, or country, or even a mid-size company. I'd argue you're only a fragmented group of fractured, warring fiefdoms vying for dominance on a planet dying under the weight of your ignorance and hatred, but I'm often called both a realist and a curmudgeon.

I believe the proper term is misanthrope, but so you might find many women after Dobbs destroyed their past, present, and future. Gee, what's left? Ah, *everyone's* past, present, and future because the only way you can birth your damn species is the women you just stole their own bodies from. Mmmm. Dumb.

Evidently, what can never be achieved is an advancement in perspective. What can never be tried, quite obviously, is some type of evolution in behavior. What will never be attempted is a societal-scale course correction about both the desire and ability to hurt people. And get away with that hurt, over and over and over again. And you'll call that inevitable, natural, "just the way it is". Then bring God into it.

Then, cue whatever rando right-wing hate profiteer is on some platform Congress doesn't have the guts to shut down, then cue the FBI at the next mass-shooting that some right-wing brainwashed guy at the edge of sanity says the platform told him to do. Lather, rinse, repeat. While women lose their jobs and their savings to cross state lines to try to get an abortion after being brutalized by some dick the law just won't catch up with. Lather, rinse, repeat.

Really? That is modern or updated or advanced? For all the tech, I'm talking about your behavior. Your beliefs. Your public discourse. That's a superior society that thinks it's sorted so much out, because, after all, what...it has low water washing machines now? That women still mostly use more than men. Yeah, check out those studies about who is still doing more housework and whose careers took a bath in the pandemic while you expect those very same people to be the larger part of bathing your own conscience in some salve after you've made them less than some sack of cells under the law.

All this assisted, endorsed, system-supported violence, poverty, and legalized traps of where the spiders want to keep us in the web. All the better to feed off of us later. Antediluvian attitudes, reruns of everything we left behind already that just get rebooted as we're berated for having a grudge against a nation that declares loudly in law and paychecks that we are less than, while telling us how fortunate we are, how grateful we should be. If this is what you call progress, then call me Miss Construed.

The hash of warped concepts you're slinging at me here about our sci-fi superpowers that seem only to promote complete destruction in what you have laughably referred to as the "twenty-first century" (oh, how I beg to differ!) sounds more like indifference and complete B.S. to me, and I have an inkling those might be optional. We can invent more gadgets all we want, but what are we spreading with them? I feel like all we're doing is creating high-tech hate toilets and flushing the nation down the drain in the process.

Have you noticed the hate toilets have an accessory range, easily customizable for any modern American anti-sanitation device? Oh, it's the accessories that seem to just match and fold and be so easily stored. They're handy to break out when you have a mess on your hands and so convenient for when you host guests.

You'll find our line of Apathy, Denial, and Patronizing Over-privileged Arrogant Cowardice is easily affordable for many retirees and six-figure earners ensconced in their enclaves and sticking their heads in the sand about the realities of other people that are simply inconvenient and therefore unreal to all healthy, able people and the top twenty-five per cent of the economic heap. We also offer a specialized Men's Line that we've kept affordable because we wouldn't want men to go without, given that they tend to produce more shit for our precious hate toilets.

Seriously, how many times have you heard it? Things like "the economy is booming" while you have been laughed out of job interviews for years on end, made fun of by your so-called friends and family for being the "loser" at work? How many times has someone over the age of sixty told you they don't care because they won't be around, while they book another round of golf at their third vacation home? How many times were we all told that reproductive rights "wouldn't be that big of a deal" because there were going to be over-the-counter medications? WHAT HAVE YOU SOLVED ABOUT WHO AND WHAT YOU CARE ABOUT?! Or, for that matter, can even admit to as fact in someone else's far worse life than yours. That you probably helped to make worse.

Invent a machine for that, geniuses. You have already, but we'll see how much of the audience gets that before the punchline.

You see, the "we just can't" that accompanies all the trendy hate is an old chestnut that's been around so long, you may not notice it on all of your devices in contrast to the louder, flashier fireworks of vitriol. But it's available to you at the click of a button, too.

All this nonsense-speak of what we can't possibly change about gender or poverty or destroying the planet or obliterating each other seems in stark contrast to how much you've actually ever even tried. At scale. In law. For a long and longer damn time. As a nation, together.

Then they get angry, don't they, when we question how much has really been taken care of because we're not as blown away and as simperingly grateful as you would have thought just because we have more soap choices. Who is using the damn soap more, though?!

It doesn't matter, big to small, there's always an excuse from those who are unaffected or those who are just plain shit as human beings. Bad things happen, bad people will always exist. Blah blah blah, motherfucker, what are we planning on *doing* about it?

I mean, don't you keep actively making it that way? Bad. There's profit to be had for some if they can make you believe that solving large-scale problems is impossible, idealistic, just stupid to try. There's the support of all the hate in turning away from change. How come that's never a crime? Isn't so much of the endless money and power you brag about having in this self-styled superpower just used to damage, divide, and drag us all down over and over again? Don't you just try very hard to say that certain changes are never possible while also promising us space jet skis, meditating our way to lottery winnings, and an eventual rebalancing where somehow we'll get our rights, someday one day?

I don't want your fucking space jet ski. I want the New Age to be old news and the headlines to be about my living wages. And "eventually" is not acceptable. Someday can kiss my ass. I want my right to choose. NOW. I'm tired of magical thinking about practical matters that have large-scale systemic problems inherent in them, and I want the change on your freaking dime instead of mine, for once. I had my right to choose, and so many promises of prosperity just a short damn American while ago. I guess that's too futuristic a concept for you to handle. Or is just too much basic human decency to allow?

Because here's the truth: the things are easy. That's the simple part. That's the part these bipedal grabby little opposable-thumbed primates think they're a bunch of gods for doing since the dawn of their species. But what would be truly revolutionary would be no such things-focused definition of advancement. It would be an advancement in thought, feeling, and behavior toward one another.

For all your upright gait, for all your grasping digits, for all your structures and tools, what really changes? Humans don't just invent tools, humans are tools. My god, have you met the bastards?! Weapons. Angels. Obstacles. Pathways. Oh, humans can do it all, but wtf are they really doing *with* it all? Humans enacting the definition of "humane" at a mass scale seems to continually elude us at a societal level. So, what part of our capacities are we truly using well? Meh.

Would you not rate us "worst species ever"? Hint: our fan club mostly consists of pesticide-resistant cockroaches, coked-up bears, and Twinkie-addicted diabetic racoons. We destroy each other and every other species besides, and possibly the capacity of an entire planet to sustain any life, while congratulating ourselves on being the pinnacle of the besty bestest best thing ever as we claim, anytime anyone wants to stop being hurt by someone else, that this is just the way it is and there's nothing we can do about that but you can absolutely have a more energy-efficient toaster if you'd like. Holy. Shit. The scale of fail is staggering, so pardon me while I puke.

There is no evolution in thought that we'll entertain in our minds long enough, level enough, and widespread enough to really change the game, hey? We're just going to keep heaping more password sign-ins for more platforms on top of mentalities defrosted and served up in microwaved Tupperware from maybe the Einsenhower era?

WE CAN'T ALL LIVE THIS WAY AND STILL LIVE. AT ALL. But some ill-defined entity unborn gets to turn my life into a 50s sitcom on twenty-first century hate roids while I'm told one more time on a disappearing planet to...*download your fucking update for the third time this week?* While simultaneously paying higher tolls for the highways of your modern robber barons who you refuse to put limits on as my body is limited in law in a way that theirs never has been and never will be?

America: please, go fuck yourself. I'm tired of you fucking me over.

Real innovation is never about technology. It is always about perspectives and behavior in how we relate with each other. Across gender lines, across state lines, across political lines, across the whole damn world.

It's only the whole damn world at stake as you force rape victims to bring more people into it. Because people are clearly a great answer to people problems.

What invention solves this problem? None of them. Everything we need to combat the viciousness of culture, the inequity of law, the purpose-crafted cruelty of stratified societies on the edge of their own annihilation in the eternal quest for an earth-swallowing "more", as long as that "more" can be yours and no one else's...there is no machine for that, analog or digital.

There is only us. The problem is the answer, and we may not be capable or willing to act on the distress signal. As with the horror genre, the call is coming from inside the house. Made by us, to us, without much of an "us" in response. Us dipshit humans who have fucked up so much there may be no turning back. Us dumbass Americans in our delusions of superiority and invincibility, convinced that somehow, somewhere, some dick-swinging self-obsessed so-called genius will invent a way out of our own accountability and pain. Our own responsibilities to, for example, "do unto others".

Your morays, your forays, your numbered days, America. Maybe it's time you "downloaded" an entirely new type of *non-technological* update that could actually help fix...anything?

Acknowledgements

L.C., the trusty beta test.

My newsletter list, for hanging in there.

And for those who read beyond the box, between the lines, and keep having the guts to go indie.

About the Author

Amy A. DeCew has done a few different things with her life but finds them all completely irrelevant to actually making a living. Between fighting for decades for medical care she still can't get and researching how to escape the United States, she's busy going rogue in a self-published context while waging a campaign against the elimination of the Oxford comma.

You can generally find her only if you hang out in international hostels because often enough, she doesn't even know what country she's in anymore. And she's probably not going to tell you, either, if all you're offering her is minimum wage.

The saucy author's backpages include stints in academic and research work, the fashion industry, and the eternal nonexistence of freelance writing. She's also appeared on stage and screen, often in disguise, and always in "the short role".

If she has to launch one more career/side hustle/part-time gig, she would like your expert crowdsourced input and/or a baseball bat to the head. Then again, maybe we'd all just like better policy-making.

Should you wish to find this Amy character, it's best to visit her website www.amydecew.online where you can discover more information about her life and work. If you're daring, you can even contact her or join her newsletter.